WALL ST. JERK

a billionaire/bbw romance

THE CURVES OF WALL ST.

MEGAN WADE

Copyright © 2021 by Megan Wade

All rights reserved.

No part of this book may be reproduced in any form or by any electronic or mechanical means, including information storage and retrieval systems, without written permission from the author, except for the use of brief quotations in a book review.

❦ Created with Vellum

BECCA

Rolling out of bed, I squint against the bright sunlight as I sit on the edge of my mattress and groan into my hands. I should never have stayed up until 5 A.M. knitting a sweater when my normal bedtime is 9 P.M. Nothing is pretty in the morning after a binge, and since I'm skating on thin ice with my supervisor already, I imagine today could be the day it's all over for me. *If only admin work didn't bore me stupid.*

Dragging my feet across the cool floor, I trudge my way into the kitchen and drop a pod inside my Keurig, shoving my favorite mug—handmade with 'knit happens' painted on it—underneath the spout in preparation for the flow of wake-me-up juice that's about to pour into it.

"Dad had better love this," I say to myself as I pick up the finished sweater from my kitchen table and hold it aloft for inspection. The cable design he chose is probably the most difficult pattern I've tackled yet, and the cashmere yarn cost me a bomb to boot. But since it's a sixtieth birthday present for the best man I know, I can't really gripe about it too much. And what's even better is that I got it finished in time to give it to him at dinner tonight. The all-nighter I pulled will have been worth it when I see the joy on his face once I hand it over. He's going to love it.

My father has a great love of handmade gifts—the mug was a result of his latest pottery class—because he considers the time and effort put into creating more valuable than any gift you can buy at the store. To him, throwing money at something is easy. He likes that the things you make are a one-of-a-kind labor of love. And as I set the sweater into the tissue-lined gift bag, I'm inclined to agree. The mug he made for me is my favorite, not because of the funny knitting pun, but because my dad made it specifically for me with his own two hands. Sure, it's slightly wobbly, and if I fill it too high it rocks and splashes coffee out the side of it. But there's just something really special about it. It was thoughtful.

Setting the gift to the side, I turn back to my coffee just as it finishes brewing, a buzzing spurt and a warm scent filling the air telling me that clear-headed reality is about to be mine.

Splashing just the right amount of milk on top so as not to cause a spill, I take my first warming sip just as my phone buzzes against the counter, a text from my work bestie, Nina, lighting up the screen.

Continuing my leisurely caffeine imbibition, I disconnect the charging cord one-handed then swipe my thumb across the screen, the words, **where the hell are you?** popping up and prompting me to frown because as far as I'm aware I don't have to be anywhere besides drinking coffee in my kitchen right now.

Scrolling back a little, I find a series of text messages inquiring as to my whereabouts before telling me the meeting is about to start. *What meeting? It's 7:00 o'clock in the bloody—oh shit.* The moment my eyes land on the time I realize I have severely fucked up.

It's not seven. It's *eleven*.

Which means I somehow slept through my alarm —*again*—probably due to the fritzy electric in this crappy apartment building. Which means I am now so incredibly late that I missed the monthly team meeting. *Which means* my absence will have been more than noted. And with performance reviews coming up, this couldn't have come at a worse time. *Shit, shit, fuckity, shit!* I was really counting on getting a raise this year. I wanted to use it to finance a move into a better apartment with amenities that actually work and a super who doesn't look at me like he's just *waiting* for me to need his 'help'. Just the idea of that sweaty, gold-toothed smile sends a shiver up and down my spine.

Fuck my life. I'm going to be stuck in the dungeon/admin pool earning a pittance forever.

Groaning, I down my coffee and type back, asking her to cover for me because I'm stuck on the subway. A tiny white lie that will have to suffice because telling them that my body clock is out of whack because I was knitting all night isn't really going to cover my ass. Neither is the fact that my electric went out. Most people set alarms on their cell phones these days and my stubborn refusal to do so means I rely on a very old analog clock because it's the only thing that's loud and obnoxious enough to get me out of bed each morning. I sleep right through my gentle, musical cell alarm, but my trusty eighties clock's bleating gets the job done ninety-nine percent of the time. The other one percent is slowly becoming the reason my boss is likely to fire me. I really can't win.

When I get a **hurry!** texted back, I dump my phone in my bag and set about throwing on the first work-appropriate outfit I can find—a knee-length plaid skirt, a white blouse, a fawn sweater vest I knitted in the fall, and a pair of black loafers—then race out the door while still brushing my hair. My makeup of basic mascara and lip gloss gets done in the subway car, and I pull my unruly dark curls into a tight bun just as I walk into the building that houses Pierce Goodman, the wealth-building company I work for. With barely a breath of air in my lungs, I burst into the meeting room with excuses at the ready, only to find it empty save for the last person I wanted to run into—my boss.

Matilde Moonen is a stern Dutch woman who's heavily accented, so whenever she's unhappy with me, I feel like a little kid in the headmaster's office, close to tears.

"Nice of you to grace us with your presence, Rebecca," she says, closing her laptop and lifting cool blue eyes my way.

"I'm so sorry. I was stuck on the—"

"Subway. I know. Unfortunately for you, you'll need to make up the missed hours since you don't have any more Paid Time Off."

"That's fine. I'll work through lunch and stay back half an hour each day for the rest of the week."

"No need to tell me. You can discuss making up your hours with Ronan." Wait. What?

My hand flies to the base of my throat. *Oh no.* "R-Ronan?" I gulp. "As in . . . Ronan Kennedy?"

"The very one." I really don't like where this is heading.

"*The* Ronan Kennedy?" AKA the devil on the top floor.

The instigator of mental breakdowns.

The career killer!

"Is there another?"

OK, OK, he isn't the literal devil, and there's no real killing involved. But by all reports, he's a nightmare to work for. Since making partner, he's gone through assistants as fast as a teenage boy goes through Kleenex. No one can adequately meet his demands and they either quit from the stress or he fires them for being incompetent. It's gotten so bad that management has started pulling people out of the admin pool to keep up with demand, and it looks like I'm this month's sacrifice—*where's Katniss to volunteer as tribute when you need her?*

"And why do I need to discuss my hours with . . . ah . . . Mr. Kennedy?" I swallow hard.

"Because there was a vote, and you weren't here to decline your nomination."

"My n-nomination? Who nominated me?"

Matilde chuckles as she rises from her chair. I don't think I'm getting that information. "You'll need to report to him immediately, Rebecca. And be warned, he doesn't react well to tardiness. But you're a fast worker and a quick learner, so maybe that'll make up for it."

"One can only hope," I wheeze, already sweating profusely as I turn away to go and face my doom.

OK. So, Ronan Kennedy is my new boss. I can handle that. I'm adaptable. And sure, I was barely getting by with my old boss, and now I have to face the man who's known to fire assistants on a whim, but I'll be OK. Surely. *Gulp.*

Oh God. Who am I kidding? I'm fucked! Who cares if I'm a "fast worker" and a "quick learner?" Ronan isn't going to give a shit about that if I'm always late. It's time to take some drastic measures to ensure I never sleep through my alarm again. I know exactly what I have to do.

RONAN

"Where the hell is my assistant?" I demand when I walk into my office and there's no one at the desk outside. It's almost midday and the phone is ringing off the hook, the message light blinking like mad. There probably hasn't been anyone manning the phone all morning. I pick the phone up and put it straight back down again. I'm so sick and tired of the incompetent staff in this place. I don't have time to deal with the ridiculous call volume myself, which is why I have an assistant in the first place. So, *whatever-her-name-is* had better have a damn good excuse or she won't have a job anymore.

"Are you talking about Rosa?" one of my analysts, Scott, asks as he follows me in to discuss the critical issues facing the company we just took a pitch meeting with.

I shake my head and frown as the phone starts up

again, the noise getting to me. "I don't know what her name is. The one with the . . . the braids," I grunt, gesturing to my own short, professionally styled blond hair as I pick the phone up and put it back down *again*. If it's important they'll call back later—hopefully when I don't have to answer it myself.

"That's Rosa. And you fired her yesterday."

I stop moving and drop my weight into the high-back chair behind my desk, clasping my hands across my chest as I do. "I did?"

"Yep."

"Huh." I have zero recollection of doing this. But then, I've fired a lot of people over the last few months so it's no surprise they're all starting to blur into one.

I used to think I was a fairly patient man. After all, I worked my way from absolutely nothing to become one of the most renowned venture capitalists on Wall Street, advancing through the ranks to make partner before most of my peers made associate. I'm in an enviable position. But while more responsibility means more rewards, it also means more stress. And ever since making partner, I've realized that my patience is rather thin.

Back when I was just a budding analyst, the only thing I had to worry about was me and my targets. But now that I'm the one on top, there's a hell of a lot more at stake—my ass and my bottom line are dependent upon the quality of my team. So if my team fails, I fail. And one thing I can tell you for certain is that Ronan Kennedy is no failure. No way. No how. I've worked too hard to be brought down by a bunch of silver-spoon carrying trust-fund kids whose daddies paid for their college.

"You don't remember firing her?"

"It might help for you to jog my memory."

Scott frowns like he's not sure if I'm serious. Then he jumps when the phone rings again. I'm quick to pick it up and leave it off the hook this time. My eyes remain on Scott expectantly. He clears his throat.

"She, uh, put the CEO from a company whose proposal you refused to fund through to you," he says, and I instantly remember. That was definitely a fireable offense. "Poor girl left in tears."

"Poor girl?" I scoff, leaning forward to rest my elbows on the desk. "Do you have any idea how much time that mistake cost the company in wasted time? I was on the phone for over an *hour* listening to that guy lament the decision I made not to fund his business idea. That's an hour I could have spent looking into proposals from entrepreneurs who actually have something worth investing in. I am not the complaints department. I am the man who decides who gets a chance and who doesn't. And that mistake cost her hers. Time is money, Scott, and I don't take kindly to having mine wasted."

"Understood," he says, moving to sit in the chair across from me. "Let's hope the next girl they send up is better at screening those calls then."

"Yes. Just like I hope *you've* gotten better at looking

into the players behind *this* proposal," I say, gesturing to the tablet he holds in his hands.

Sweat beads on his upper lip as he clears his throat. It's well known that I have high expectations when it comes to this game and those who work under me. I want my team to have their ear so close to the ground that they can look at a proposal and know on instinct whether it's a good investment or not. Then I want them researching the fuck out of it, finding all of the dirt on every single person with an iota of power involved. Then I want to know the technical details of the products, a breakdown of all competition, and an estimate of the market demand. All so that when they sit across from me and tell me why we should invest, they have one hundred percent confidence that backing this project will be a win for Pierce Goodman and for our team. I expect my team to be as hungry as I am, and if they don't measure up, well, out the door they go. Assistants. Analysts. I don't care what role you play, disappoint me—get in my way—and you're gone.

"I have," he says, swallowing hard as he swipes at his screen. "And I think you'll be pleasantly surprised with what I've found."

BECCA

"I am so totally jealous of you right now," Nina says, a wistful expression on her face as she watches me pull my things from my desk drawer and drop them into a cardboard box. I don't have a huge amount of personal stuff adorning my desk, but there are a handful of photos, a cute little cactus, a couple of pattern books I like to browse through, and of course I have my knitting bag. That's something I don't go anywhere without. I'd rather knit with just my fingers than sit around with nothing to do but make idle chit chat if I'm honest.

"Jealous of the fact that I'm going to have to start looking for a new job before long?" I ask, glancing up at her as I set my green and red cactus on top of my belongings so it doesn't get squashed or damaged. "In case you haven't noticed, most of the girls who go up to the top floor only last a couple of months, and they don't come back down here again. They're out on their ass. And I for one, can't afford to do that. I barely have any savings as it is."

Twirling side to side in her desk chair, Nina flicks her blonde hair over her shoulder and lets out a longing sigh. "I think I'd happily look for another job if it meant I got to spend one on one time in the presence of Ronan Kennedy."

"Nina, I don't think you're hearing me. I'm worried for my employment status here."

"Oh, I hear you. But, have you seen that man up close?" She fans at herself dramatically. "I was in the elevator alone with him once, and I all about self-combusted from his gorgeousness alone. It should be a sin to be *that* good-looking *and* that wealthy."

"Pity it doesn't make him a nicer person," I say, slinging my purse over my head so it sits across my chest. "Did you even see Rosa on her way out yesterday? She was a sniveling mess and couldn't stop calling him *El Diablo*. I don't know about you, but I don't have sympathy for any devils—no matter *how* good-looking or rich they are."

Nina blows out a raspberry and waves her hand in the air dismissively. "I doubt he's *that* bad. Besides, Rosa was always prone to dramatics. Remember that time she cried over the printer jamming?"

"Yeah. I do. And she was eight months pregnant at the time, and the entire toner cartridge exploded all over her white shirt. So, I think we can forgive her that one."

"Sure," she says, with the bounce of her shoulder. "I still don't think it could be that bad working for him, though. Especially for you, because you're a gun."

"A gun?"

"Yeah. Like, you blow through all of your work faster than a normal person. It's why you've gotten more chances from Matilde than the rest of us combined."

"I really don't think that's true," I mutter, hefting the box into my arms. "I've been on thin ice around here for a while."

"And yet *you're* the one who got chosen by the powers that be for a promotion."

"Promotion," I scoff. "More like a banishment. I'll be lucky if I last more than a month. And before you get all swoony over the man again, Rosa isn't the only ex-employee with a nightmare story to tell about Ronan Kennedy. He's been on the top floor for less than a year and he's already gone through *six* assistants. And God knows how many analysts he's gotten rid of in his quest for the perfect team. By all accounts, the man is highly strung and has a temper to boot. So, I suggest you take a good look at this"—I use my index finger to circle around my face—"because it won't be around much longer."

"You know what? I don't believe that. I think this is the role that's going to turn everything around for you. Just think, if you can make it just six months as Ronan's assistant, the extra money will not only build your savings, but it will also give you the chance to move out of that shitty apartment building that I swear should be condemned by now." Nina found a dead rat in the stairwell once and has refused to visit me at my apartment ever since. I shudder at the memory because honestly, I don't blame her. I've lost count of the dead rats I've found. Not to mention the roaches. I want out too.

"Six months?" With a raised-brow sigh, I slip my fingers through the handle of my knitting bag and balance it swinging beneath the box. "I think pulling that off would take some kind of Christmas miracle, and since it's now January, it's too late for that."

"You're going to do great, Becca. I have the utmost faith in you!"

"Faith. OK. Well, how about we catch up for lunch tomorrow and I'll tell you how far that faith is getting me?" I suggest as I step away from my old desk, butterflies flitting around in my belly at the idea of heading toward my new one on the thirty-fifth floor.

Nina's eyes light up. "Yes! And you can tell me all about your new boss in *great detail*." She waggles her brows, and I can't help but laugh as I take one last look around then head for the elevators.

"Knock 'em dead, babe!" she calls after me when the doors open and I step inside. I throw a half-hearted smile over my shoulder then swallow down my nerves as I hit the button for the top floor and ready myself for what's to come. I'm glad Nina has faith in me because all I have is a great sense of dread. While I was hoping to get a raise this month, becoming the executive assistant to

Wall Street's biggest jerk wasn't the kind of leg up I had in mind.

Just as the elevator doors close, my cell buzzes in my purse to tell me I have a message. I do a slight balancing act to get to it, and when I hold it up, a text from Nina fills the screen: **Take pictures! Lots and lots of his forearms and his ass :drooling emoji:**

Rolling my eyes, I drop my cell back into my bag, the dread feeling a little less poignant as I laugh at my friend's antics while the elevator makes its climb. Unfortunately, the trip from admin to the top floor is shorter than expected. And when I step out, it's to the sound of none other than Ronan Kennedy, doing what Ronan Kennedy does best—yelling.

"Research? This is nothing more than a pathetic lack of effort. Do it again. And if it's not done to my satisfaction by the time I leave this office tonight, I don't want you to bother coming back tomorrow."

Gritting my teeth, I take a deep breath and force my feet to move, one in front of the other. It feels a lot like one of those scenes in a gangster movie where the bad guy gives someone a shovel and tells them to start digging. In this instance, I'm the one with the shovel and with every step that takes me closer to Ronan Kennedy's office, I'm digging my grave a little deeper.

RONAN

"Don't just look at me, Scott. Get the fuck out and get to work," I snap, causing my analyst to turn and scurry out of my office with his head down, tablet tucked under his arm.

With a discontented sigh, I turn away to look out the window, trying to talk myself down so I don't go out there and fire every single person on my team for letting him walk in here underprepared. They should be looking out for each other. But instead, they're all too focused on themselves to have any kind of idea what real teamwork is.

I know I have a reputation for being a hard ass, but I'd rather that than have a single member of my staff thinking they can walk all over the top of me or turn in half-assed work. And so what if I have a high staff turnover and send people cowering whenever I walk into a room? My methods get results. It's *because* of my reputation that we're the one team in the company with our projects all in the black.

That's more than I can say for Pete Greer down the hall. He got made partner a year before I did, and last month one of the projects he invested in went bankrupt. The senior partners are livid, and I'm just over here with an 'I told you so' smirk because it was a deal I refused. After looking into the management team, I found someone with a sketchy financial past and put the deal in the discard pile immediately. They say everyone deserves a second chance, but people who don't know how to manage their money tend to repeat the same mistakes time and time again. I need to see evidence of them righting their wrongs before I'll allocate any of the funds to them that I have a say over. In this guy's case, I was right to pull back. Pete, though, he has a thing about trying to prove he's better than me, and sometimes that competitiveness causes him to make dumb calls.

Due diligence is *everything* in this game. If you don't know what you're investing in, you don't know your risk. It's why I'm so hard on my team, and it's why management lets me get away with being heavy-handed with the pink slips. Still, there's only so much leeway I can take advantage of. And firing my entire team in one go might be the thing that pushes me over the line and gets *me* fired. And since I really like earning the big bucks, I might hold off another day or two.

"My cactus!" My head snaps around when I hear a

yelp, prefaced by a clattering of things scattering across the floor.

"Shit. I'm so sorry," Scott bumbles, kneeling just outside my door in front of the dowdiest dressed woman I've ever seen. He scrambles to pick up the balls of yarn that are skittering and unraveling across the floor. *Wait. Yarn?* Who the fuck brings yarn to Wall St? Little grannies?

Lifting my foot, I bring the tip of my shoe down on top of a wayward ball then crouch to pick it up. My fingers sink into it. It's a soft, dusty blue cashmere that is surprisingly pleasant to touch. In fact, as I wind it up and follow the yarn trail to its owner, I'm reminded of the one person in my past who gave a damn about me as a scrawny kid—my best friend's grandmother.

Granny Dee was a stern woman and an avid knitter. The click-clack of her knitting needles while Banks and I did our homework at the kitchen table with his cousin, Darren, is a sound I'll always remember with fondness. It was her relentless insistence that Banks and I better ourselves that turned me into the man I am today. The scratchy woolen sweaters she made us wear, however, are something I'd rather forget. I don't think I've owned anything knitted since I left college and got my first job.

"It's fine. I wasn't really watching where I was going either," the brunette woman with the messy bun says as she tosses her things back into a box and shakes her head despondently, scooping the soil from her plant into a broken pot.

Seeing her like that, I make the snap assumption that one of my colleagues has taken a leaf from my book and fired a team member for not being hungry enough. But then, I could tell you this girl wasn't built for Wall Street just by looking at her outfit. She's wearing loafers, a knitted sweater vest and a pleated skirt in an office where everyone else sports a smart gray or charcoal suit over a sharp white or pale blue shirt—the outfit of the serious investor who has no time for flair—and to top that off, she's sulking over a broken cactus pot and spilled knitting needles. Where this girl belongs is in a library or a farmhouse in the country somewhere. The mind boggles over who in their right mind hired her here in the first place.

"I'm assuming this belongs to you," I say, holding out the now wound-up ball.

Her shoulders stiffen and she jerks her head up with a gasp, meeting my eyes with the most azure blue gaze I've ever seen.

"Please don't fire me," she whispers, slowly getting to her feet.

"Why on earth would I fire you?"

"Isn't that what you do?" Something inside me shifts and I falter slightly as she takes the yarn from my hand, I almost release it too early.

"Not without cause." I'm quick to clear my throat and regain my composure as I step back from her, unsure why her comment made me feel so off-balance. Shouldn't I be glad that my reputation precedes me?

"I'm knitting a scarf," she blurts suddenly, her eyes flicking down as she shoves the ball of yarn into a carpet bag.

"I don't recall asking," I state, annoyed at my reaction and annoyed at her for causing it. Maybe I *should* fire her? If she's worried that I'm going to, then I obviously have the power to do so. That can only mean that she's the new assistant HR had sent up. And so far, I'm not impressed. "But since you feel the need to tell me all about yourself, how about we start with a name?"

She scowls before she clears her throat and sets her spine straight, a sweet scent touching my nose as she steps closer, jutting her hand out in greeting. "Becca Maxwell. I work in admin. Well, I don't anymore. I'm to be your new executive assistant."

A slow grin curves my mouth as I look from her hand to her, my eyes taking in the mousey girl with the amazing eyes and more curves than a woman dressed so matronly has a right to.

"They sent *you* up *here?*" I question, my hands sliding into my pockets as my grin turns into a chuckle. "To be *my* assistant?" I take another step back and shake my head. "You know what, you were right in the beginning. This isn't going to work. Go back down there and tell them to send someone else." I spin on my heel and head back into my office, suddenly feeling lightheaded. *Does she smell like . . . jellybeans?*

"And what's so wrong with me?" she demands, following me in with an adorably indignant jut of her chin. "I'm just as capable as anyone else down there, if not more so. I'm probably the fastest and most efficient admin assistant they have. I'm also great at communicating, and I'm excellent at leading and working as part of a team. So, you don't get to take one look at me and make a judgment about what you think I can and can't do because you'll be wrong, and I'll prove it. I don't know if you have something against me being a woman or if you just have something against me being fat. But I'm pretty sure that no matter how you look at that, turning me away at this point counts as either wrongful termination or discrimination at best."

"It has nothing to do with either of those things," I growl, reeling because this confrontation has gone from a nuisance blip in my day to turning me the fuck on. "I simply don't want an assistant who's too clumsy to get out of the way when someone's walking right at her. In this job, I expect every member of my team to have their wits about them at all times. You very obviously do not."

"Then what about him out there?" she demands, holding her hand out and gesturing toward Scott who's now holding her box and knitting bag and gaping at us. "Is he fired too?"

Scott's eyes bulge, and he looks like he wants to dive behind something and hide.

"He's on his final warning," I say, noting the visible relief in the set of his shoulders as he puts the items on the nearest desk and scurries away, probably hoping that if he stays out of my way he'll be safe. *Good luck with that, buddy.*

"Then I think the very least you can do is let me have a warning too. Not that having some guy slam into me when I was waiting outside your door is in any way my fault, mind you. But since I just got this job and I don't feel like explaining to my slimy landlord why I can't make rent this month, I'd appreciate it if I could be judged on my work and not my ability to dodge obstacles."

My eyes narrow slightly as the words *slimy* and *landlord* burrow their way into my brain, causing long since buried memories to rise to the surface. As I push them away, a sense of protectiveness surges inside me—something I was too young to provide when it was my mother on the slimy receiving end. It causes the hairs on the back of my neck to stand on end. *If he or any man ever dares to make her feel uncomfortable, I will rain hell upon them.* I honestly have zero clue where all this is coming from. Normally, I can find a woman attractive and do nothing about it. But in Becca's case, something about her looks combined with her fire, combined with her tapping into something from my past is making me feel all kinds of unwanted things. Many of them completely inappropriate for the workplace. This reaction to a woman—any woman—is new, and I'm not quite sure how to handle it besides get away from her as fast as I possibly can. But she's right. I can't fire her based on looks alone. I have to let her do the job first. *Shit.*

"Fine." I have to swallow a massive lump in my throat

before I can even talk. "Set yourself up at the desk outside my office. Gatekeep both the phone and my door. I don't want to be interrupted for the rest of the day. Understood?"

Blinking rapidly, she sucks in a deep, lung filling breath that only accentuates the size of her chest as she nods. "I can do that. Anything else?"

"Don't fuck up," I say, standing there with my teeth clenched tight as she whispers an OK, then turns and saunters out of my office, her head held high and her ass swaying so hypnotically my balls ache. The moment she takes a seat at her desk, I stalk over to the door and slam it closed, taking in gulp after gulp of air as I try to figure out what the hell just went on.

BECCA

"Oh wow, pumpkin. This is just . . . I love it," Dad says, holding the newly unwrapped sweater up at dinner that night. "Absolutely love it. In fact, I'm going to put it on right now."

I giggle as I sit across from him, watching him pull his current sweater off and replace it with the new one. It makes his salt and pepper gray hair stand up and almost takes his glass of wine out in the process.

"How do I look?" he says, holding his arms out to the side.

"You look like you just rolled out of bed, but I'm glad you like it," I reply, reaching across the table and doing my best to make him look presentable again. One thing I can say for my father is that he's a big goof and doesn't care who knows it. When I was a kid, he would happily sit for hours while I used him as my beauty shop customer, letting me paint his nails, style his hair, and apply any number of colorful cosmetics to his face. We'd get parcels and he'd just answer the door looking like a clown, but he acted like it was nothing out of the ordinary before returning to our game. Most of my best memories involve this man. He's the standard by which I hold all others.

"It's perfect. So soft too. You shouldn't have gone to so much expense. I know this kind of yarn doesn't come cheap. I'd love this just for the time you put into it."

"I know. But you're worth it, Dad. You only turn sixty once, and since I just got a promotion at work, I think I can more than afford to splurge a little," I say with a wink, putting on a brave face to hide the fact that I spent the entire day feeling beyond miserable. Ronan barely said a word to me all afternoon, preferring to interact with grunts and harrumphs. And to top it off, he stayed behind in the office, expecting me to be his gatekeeper for so long that I barely made it here on time for our reservation. I almost missed my dad's birthday because of that jerk. He is just the worst, and I don't know how I'm going to make it longer than a few days in this job, let alone the six months Nina thinks I'm capable of. It'll take a miracle of perseverance, that's for sure. But to be safe, I think I'll start browsing job listings in preparation for the day when Ronan's moodiness gives me my marching orders. He's got the entire first floor on edge.

"A promotion, you say? Does this mean you'll be working closer to your brother?" Dad leans his elbows on the table and gives me his undivided attention.

"Possibly. I didn't see him today, but from the whispers I heard in the break room, one of his projects fell through and he's working double-time to prove himself. I imagine he'll be in a bear of a mood when I see him next."

"Hmm." Dad finishes his mouthful and mops at his mouth with a napkin. "He was thinking of joining us for dinner tonight, but he couldn't get away. Had a gift couriered to me, though. Fancy watch." He lifts his brow and extends his arm, showing me the Rolex hanging slightly loose on his boney wrist.

"You don't like it?"

Dad shrugs. "It's fine. I just feel funny having something so expensive dangling on the end of my arm. Your brother has never really understood my stance on gift giving. Same as your mother. She always enjoyed the bling."

"He means well. To him, getting you a top-of-the-line watch *is* being thoughtful."

"He values money over time. But when money isn't worth a thing, time will *always* be precious."

"I get it, Dad. And Peter will too. He's just caught up in the thick of it now. Once he's finally settled down and started a family of his own, maybe he'll see things differently."

"I doubt it. He's his mother's son. But teaching one kid out of two how to value time isn't so bad, right?"

"I suppose," I say, giving him a small smile while I bite my tongue because I don't want to say anything to upset him on his birthday. I love my dad to bits, but ever since Mom left him for another man after I went away to college, he's struggled with anything that reminds him of her—especially Peter because he's the most like her in both looks and personality. So, what was already a tenuous father-son relationship became even more strained under the weight of his disappointment. Peter feels like he can't win. Dad feels like he isn't understood. And I feel caught in the middle of it all.

"How about you tell me about this job of yours," Dad says, thankfully changing the subject while he spears some pasta on the end of his fork.

"Well, it's on the top floor, so I get an amazing view of the city whenever I'm in the break room. And it's as an executive assistant to one of the partners. Double my current salary. Not sure of the perks yet. But it's a big leg up."

"Does it mean you can get out of that apartment?" he asks, brows raised.

"Eventually."

"I honestly just wish you'd come back home and commute on the ferry each day."

"I know, Dad. And I know my apartment is the pits. But I like being in the city."

"It's not your apartment I have a problem with—although, it could definitely be improved. My problem is with that landlord of yours. I don't like the way he looks at you." Me either. But I do take heart in the fact that he looks at all the women that way, young or old, big or small. When Dad met him for the first time, he insisted I install a slide bolt and a second deadlock then checked every corner of my apartment to make sure there weren't any hidden cameras. There weren't but Vince definitely gives off major creep vibes.

"I keep away from him as much as possible, I promise. But, yes, I'll definitely be moving as soon as I've saved enough and found somewhere decent."

"Precisely why you shouldn't have gone to this expense," he says, gesturing to the beautifully soft cashmere of his new sweater.

"Oh, Dad. Don't start with this. Please? It's your birthday and I just wanted to do something special for you. I promise I'm frugal every other day of the year. You don't need to worry about me."

"Well, I do," he says, waving his fork around with a wobbly piece of ravioli balancing on the end. "You're my only daughter, and I'm your father. Worrying about you is my job."

"And I love you for it. But tonight is all about you. I even organized your favorite for dessert—tiramisu. So, no more money talk and no more Mom talk. Got it?"

"Consider me silent," he says, miming zipping his lips before he gives me a child-like smile. Despite being the most responsible man on the planet, when it comes to anything sweet, my dad is like a little kid in a candy store. No sooner have I mentioned the rich coffee-flavored dessert and he's dropping his fork and pushing his plate away to eagerly move onto the next course.

With a smile, I raise my hand above my head and signal the waiter. "We'd like to move onto dessert, please."

"Of course, signorina. Right away."

AFTER WAVING Dad off when he got on the Staten Island ferry, I made my way back home, stopping off at a Best Buy on the way and picking up the loudest alarm clock they have with a backup battery option. The clerk assured me that this alarm wouldn't let me down in the way my old 80s analog clock has been.

As I sit on my bedside setting it up, my cell goes off with a message from my brother.

Peter: How was dinner?

Me: Pretty normal. Dad was wearing the watch you gave him :smiley face:

Peter: He hates it, doesn't he?

Me: Oh no! He's just funny about letting us spend money on him. He complained about the cost of the cashmere yarn I used on his sweater too. You did good, big bro. You still at the office?

Peter: Just leaving. Did I hear right that you've been promoted to Kennedy's assistant?

Me: You did. I don't count it as a promotion, though. It's more throwing me to the lions to see how long I last for entertainment purposes. Is there a betting pool happening yet?

Peter: Of course. :laughing emoji:

Me: Did you bet? And don't lie. I know you placed a bet.

Peter: I have my money on three months.

Me: You suck :eye roll emoji:

Peter: Maybe. Just don't let me down, OK?

I drop my phone on the bed with a sigh. He thinks three months and Nina thinks six. But jokes on them, because after today, I'll be lucky to make it to the weekend. I'm pretty sure my new boss already hates me.

RONAN

"What are you still doing here, buddy?" Banks asks in the quiet of his closed-for-the-night bar, Banked Up. It's the number one place to be for anyone who works on Wall Street. Connections and deals worth millions are made here every night over top-shelf liquor. Insights are gleaned, gossip about failed deals shared, while lessons are learned for future endeavors. It's like this magical land of financial information, and I just happen to have grown up with the owner and consider him as not only my best friend, but my family too.

"I dunno, man. I'm just not ready to move my ass off this stool."

He grabs a glass and a bottle of Grey Goose, topping me up and pouring a drink for himself before he sits down next to me.

"Did you fire your assistant again?" It's said in jest, but little does he know he's right.

"Since you asked, yes I did. But I have another one now, and I'm not sure I can work with her either." It's been less than a day, and already Becca has proven to be a massive distraction. I'm attracted to her. Ridiculously so. It took me two hours longer than normal to finish up my work because I was too busy staring out the door and imagining how she sounds when she moans, how she'd look if she were gasping beneath me. I feel like a dirty fuck because of it and ended up closing and locking my door so I wouldn't have to look at her anymore. Didn't stop me from being able to hear her, though. That woman can find joy in anything and her laugh is like a tinkling little bell. So I imagined stuffing her panties in her mouth to muzzle her and that just set me off all over again.

"Jesus, Ronan. You're never gonna find yourself a decent assistant if you don't give them time to learn the ropes. What's wrong with this one?"

I grit my teeth and look into my glass, dragging a hand through my dark blond hair before I meet Banks's dark eyes with a sigh. "You wouldn't understand."

"That's where you're wrong, my friend. Because I do understand. You demand excellence, and anyone who's not as infallible as you think *you* are, isn't worth your time." That's only part of it.

"Guess you understand just fine," I lie, tipping back my drink and finishing it in one gulp. While Banks is my closest friend, there's no way I'm telling him I'm chomping at the bit over my new assistant. Not only is my interest totally inappropriate with our current power dynamic, but I also don't ever go mental over women—especially one that I only just met. The fact it happened so suddenly over a woman most would describe as 'dowdy' bothers me.

"You forget that I understand what you're going through more than most," Banks continues, still talking about the stress of the job and not my inability to control my dick around the new girl. "It's why I got out of the game and invested in myself for a change. It was a risk, but I'm so much better off mentally for getting out of that place. And if I hadn't left, I probably never would have met Isla. Pursuing her was a risk. But when you follow your heart and bet on yourself, you can't lose."

Banks and I not only grew up and went through school together, but we both worked at Pierce Goodman straight out of college too. The difference between us is that when Banks got stupid rich, he cashed out and funded his dream of opening a bank-themed bar to match his name. For me, my dream was only to *be* stupid rich. And I'm not sure at what point my bank balance is going to feel like enough for me. Maybe a few more zeros will do it?

"So, what you're saying is that you think I should throw in the towel on everything I've worked toward and invest in myself because it will lead me to the woman of my dreams?"

He grins. "Crazier things could happen."

"I don't even know what I'd do. The only game I know is venture capital. And I'm on track to make senior partner in the next year."

Banks shrugs as he sips his drink. "Why be senior partner when you can be the sole owner? Start your own firm. There's no one to stop you going out on your own. You've got the capital, right?"

"I do. But then I'm the one taking on all the risk."

"Freedom has a price, buddy," he says, getting up from his stool and clapping me on the back. "I guess it just depends on how badly you want it, and how much you're willing to pay for it."

"I'm not willing to pay for anything," I say, rising from my seat. "It's why I drink here all the time. Drinks are free."

He laughs as I pull my money clip from my pocket and throw a couple of notes on the bar like I always do—I don't take handouts from anyone, even my best friend. "You're right. I've never met a freeloader quite like you, Ronan."

Giving him a wink, I pocket my clip then head for the door, thanking him for the chat.

"Just think about what I said," he calls after me. "It'll change your life."

I nod, but I don't really mean it. Because while I work in a high-risk environment, what I really want in life is stability, and sinking my savings into a firm of my own isn't that. Besides, if I left Pierce Goodman to go out on my own now, I'd never have the chance to get over this infatuation I have with Becca. No. If I keep her around, I'll eventually stop reacting to her. I know it. I've never had a long-term infatuation in my life. So I can't imagine this will be any different. And besides, in the time it takes me to get used to having her around without wanting to fuck her, she might actually turn out to be a decent assistant.

I guess that's something that only time will tell.

BECCA

"What's his mood like today?" Scott asks in a whisper, nervously adjusting the tie on his wiry frame as he looks into Ronan's office and gulps.

"Well, so far I've received a grunt to my good morning, and a harrumph to my request for more work," I say as I twist the cable needle to the correct position on the new scarf I'm knitting. "But he did seem to enjoy the lemon sugar muffins I made last night. So, whatever *that* means is his mood."

As happens in a lot of my jobs, I burn through the set work I'm given faster than most, which means I'm done well before lunchtime hits. Then I'm left with pretty much nothing else to do except man the phones, chase up analysts to make sure they're doing their due diligence, and deal with sporadic emails for the rest of the day. It's obscenely boring, and I've asked Ronan to give me something more to do several times over the past three months I've been working here—sorry, Pete, you lost the betting pool there—but he seems to be happy paying me to twiddle my thumbs.

I find the whole situation odd given his generally irritable temperament, but I'm not about to jump up and down and complain. So, with no work to do, I'm perfectly happy sitting here getting paid to knit. It means that when I'm home—in my *new* apartment since I got a great deal on one via some special company executive housing program that provides a car and everything—I can find new passions like baking.

Every day, I bring some new delectable treat in for the team. It's made me some fast friends, and since Ronan's firing sprees also seemed to end around the same time I started baking a month into my current role, some of my colleagues think there's magic in my muffins. But I know that's not the case because the way to Ronan's heart—or at least the way into Ronan's good graces—isn't via his stomach. It's via thorough work. Something I've been ensuring *all* his analysts do before presenting him with *anything*. And as the gatekeeper of his time, I double and triple check everyone's work before I grant them entry. I suppose you could call me the Gandalf of Wall St these days. *You shall not pass!*

As a result of the improved team performance, he isn't being as much of a bear toward me. That's not to say he's being nice to me either. More . . . indifferent, I suppose. But that suits me fine. I do my work, and when that's finished, I pull out my knitting and man the phones. In the last month alone, I've made two sweater vests and finished the scarf for myself. This new one is for the crankypants boss himself. He may be an asshole, but the fact he doesn't chew me out for knitting once my work is done is a big plus as far as I'm concerned. And I've noticed him walking in with his collar pulled up lately, so I thought making this for him could be seen as a gesture of goodwill. Maybe it will get us past the grunts and onto verbal communication? A girl can dream.

"Grunting?" Scott muses, his hand moving to rub the back of his neck. "I'll take that as a good sign because it doesn't involve yelling."

I laugh at his response, glancing up at him as I finish off the row and click my counter over. "Gotta pick your moments, right?"

"Are there any good moments where he's concerned? He isn't called the Jerk of Wall Street for nothing." He leans in and says that last part conspiratorially. I laugh.

"They really call him that?"

"Sure do. The man has quite the reputation. Hey. Wanna look over this report one last time before I go in?" he asks, handing over his tablet. "Ever since you saved my ass by picking up that mistake I missed last month, I'm petrified to go in there without showing you my research one last time. I swear he makes me so damn nervous that I overthink it all and then I end up overlooking something. You know, I used to watch Shark Tank and think picking the best projects to invest in was easy. It's really not. There's so much involved." He runs a hand over his face, his dark brown eyes looking tired and concerned.

"I guess you'll hone your instincts in time," I say, taking a couple of Kleenex from the box on my desk and offering them to him to mop his brow while I read his work. Ever since my first day on this job, Scott has been the most welcoming of the entire team, so I'm more than happy to give him a little extra help. And I think I have a pretty good handle on the things Ronan looks for in a pitch—especially when he's so vocal about his disappointment—so I can generally pick up on anything a pitch might be lacking and point it out for them to fix before they approach him.

"I don't know," he says, accepting the tissues and blowing his nose instead of wiping the sweat off his face. I try to hide my smile. "Each day that I come here, I realize there's more to learn. I don't think I'll ever be an expert at this the way Ronan is. I swear he must be some sort of robot Terminator or something. Because it's like we go into pitch meetings and he takes one look at the person presenting and instantly downloads all the information on them direct to his brain. I don't think you can learn that. It's something innate." He takes his tablet back when I hand it to him and sighs. "And all this research I do can't possibly measure up."

"Well, if it's any consolation, I think you more than covered your ass here. I remember thinking in the pitch that this guy seemed a little green but had a good head on his shoulders. You've looked into his background, his close contacts, and business associates, and he's pretty clean. If I had the money, I'd fund this for sure."

A crooked smile curves his thin lips as he straightens his spine. "I think that too. Thanks."

"No problem. Now go in there and sell your decision."

"Here's to meeting Ronan's impossible standards then," he jokes, giving me a salute. And I smile, but at the same time, I think that everything about Ronan seems impossible. Just having a conversation with him is a struggle. He's impossibly beautiful too. I'd be lying if I denied the fact that he gives me all over body tingles whenever we make eye contact. Nina wasn't lying when she pointed out how attractive he is up close. I mean, I'd seen him in the building a few times before I came to work for him. But I'd never had a reason to interact—not that I'm interacting much now either.

I know it's only been three months, but I really thought he would have warmed up to me a little by now. When I first started, I thought that maybe the lack of communication was his way of forcing me to slip up so he could fire me. But as time went by without the dramatic firing event I was expecting, I started to realize that as long as I did my work and minimized his need to micromanage as much as possible—something I do by researching projects before we hear their pitch then checking over the analysts' research before they take it to him—then he left me entirely alone. Actually, it's almost like he pretends I don't exist.

While a little uncomfortable, as far as jobs go, it's a pretty sweet deal with great perks. But I have to admit that I am a little bored, I thought this would be a high stress, challenging position. And I say as much to my brother when I meet him for a rare lunch later that same day.

"I heard about the knitting," he says, lifting his brow at me as he slurps his soup.

"Oh yeah? What are they saying?"

"That Kennedy has lost his edge. He'd never let an assistant sit there knitting sweater vests before you."

"They're seriously saying that? He's still outperforming every other partner in the VC division. Including you."

"True. But he's been gunning for senior partner, and numbers alone don't get you across that line. Weakness is a problem for the higher ups. And you, my dear sister, seem to be his."

"What? How? That's . . . that's ludicrous. Did you tell them all that I'm just really fucking fast at my job?"

"If I did, they'd all find out you were my little sister, wouldn't they?"

"True," I say with a sigh. Peter got me the job at Pierce Goodman after I lost my last one due to my tendency to oversleep—thankfully rectified with that sonic alarm I purchased—but to ensure I was never given any favoritism due to my brother being partner, I use our mother's maiden name instead of my dad's surname. That way, I'm a Maxwell and Peter is a Greer, and the two never get mixed up. "But it would be nice to know if someone was setting them straight. I don't like the idea of them talking about me like that. Or Ronan, for that matter."

"Oh, come on. You can't seriously be concerned about how they talk about Ronan? He does absolutely nothing to illicit a kind thought out of anyone. Don't go thinking just because you hold the record for not being fired that he's somehow a nice guy because of it. The man has only ever been interested in himself."

"I don't pretend to know anything about how Ronan's mind works. I just know how to stay off his shit list."

"By knitting?"

"No." I smile as I pick up a French fry and swirl it in my pot of ketchup. "By doing my job and paying attention to what he's looking for. You're just cranky because you lost the betting pool."

"Everyone is cranky because they lost the betting pool. You've disappointed us all."

"Boohoo. I'm so sorry my attention to detail failed to line your pockets."

Slurping some soup from his spoon, he narrows an eye as he swallows then licks his lips. "So you've figured out how the beast operates then?"

"There's not much to figure out. He cares only about competence," I reply simply.

His brow shoots up. "Competence?"

"Yes. But not just any old competence. He wants

everyone around him performing at a level as high as him."

"So, that's what you do? You make sure everyone on his team is performing to his standard?"

"That's exactly what I do. And I have a feeling that's the reason he lets me knit. It's not because he's losing his edge. It's because he's gained an advantage."

"And yet, you're bored?"

Biting off the end of my fry, I nod as I chew carefully. "It's true. But it's the same for all things, really. I still enjoy knitting, but I took up baking recently and I'm already getting bored with that."

He gasps in mock horror. "Are you saying that my sister, the serial hobbiest, has grown tired of yet another hobby?"

"Shocking, I know. But I'll stick with it a little longer because I recently found a cookbook called 'Baked with Heart' by a woman named Yvette Valentine. She's got a bakery in a little town called Whisper Valley and her lemon sugar muffins are simply delicious."

"What if I could offer you something a little more challenging?"

It's my turn to raise my eyebrows. "Such as?"

"A spot on my team. I know you don't have the same qualifications as most of my new hires, but you definitely have the aptitude. If you could bring that mind of yours along with everything you've learned from Ronan so far onto my team, I have a feeling we'd be unbeatable."

"Wouldn't that be a conflict of interest since we're

family and all? I thought we kept our relationship to each other quiet specifically to avoid that type of thing."

"We did. And we still will. No one has to know there's any favoritism here. As far as they're concerned, I saw what an asset you were on Kennedy's team and poached you for my own."

An uneasy feeling hits my belly and makes me put the second half of my fry down, uneaten. "I don't know, Pete. It feels a little, I don't know, dishonest. And I don't want to leave Ronan in the lurch. Especially not when the team is finally working well together. I've put a lot of effort into getting them where they are now."

"Whatever he's paying you right now, I'll double it."

"Pete."

"Triple."

"Do you even have the authority to do that?"

"Of course. As long as I bring in profit, I can do whatever needs doing. And if that means I get to make my little sister's life easier and more interesting, then that's what I'm going to do."

"Jesus. Can I think about it?"

"Of course. As long as while you think about you, you quit seeing it as abandoning Ronan and look at it as an opportunity to grow yourself."

"I can try to do that."

"Good. And while you're thinking on it, why don't you come out with me and my team tonight? There's this great bar I want you to check out. It's *the* place to be if you want to get a good feel for the financial district and see where you want this career of yours to go. We'll kick back, have a few drinks, and end a long week on a fun note."

"Oh God, Peter, you know how much I dislike going out, and I really don't drink."

"Come on, Bec. I rarely get to see my little sister as it is and maybe this is my way of trying to rectify that. Can you make an exception? Just this once?"

Letting out my sigh, I feel my head nodding before I've actually decided to agree. He's just played the one card he knows I can't resist—time with family—and before I know it, I'm agreeing to go to a cocktail bar called Banked Up.

RONAN

"Who invited Rebecca?" I demand, the hairs on the back of my neck standing on end before I even knew it was her causing it.

My analysts look between each other in confusion until Scott clears his throat. "Not me. But, maybe she heard us talking?" he suggests. "She *is* part of the team, so it makes sense she'd want to be here . . . right?" He gulps and looks around at his teammates for backup that doesn't arrive. "I mean, I think she deserves to be here."

"Perhaps," I admit, even though my eye twitches. I keep seeing him hovering around her desk, so I'm trying to gauge his interest in her. If it's anything more than collegial I'll lose my mind. "Do you think she wants to be an analyst?" My eyes stray to where she's weaving her way through the crowd, and when she locks eyes with mine, she seems surprised to see me. *Me too, sweet girl. Me too.*

A small smile curves her mouth as she lifts her hand

and gives me a little finger wave before she takes in the team, her expression turning quizzical before looking around the room searchingly. *Wait. Is she here meeting someone else? A date?*

But it couldn't be a date. She's got one of those damn pleated skirts and sweater vests on that she wears to the office. It makes her look both uptight and vulnerable, but she doesn't look date-ready, so maybe she just heard about this place in the break room and decided to check it out for herself? I wouldn't put it past her. She's not the kind of person to let information slip by her without investigating for herself. If she wasn't putting that inquisitive effort into me and my team, I'd think she'd make a great detective. Better yet, she could probably make it as a venture capitalist. Possibly even one good enough to rival me.

"An analyst? I'm not sure," Scott says. "Maybe she just wants something more to do besides knitting?"

The comment makes my eye twitch again. I like her knitting. I find the sound soothing. I like that it tells me exactly where she is and what she's doing at any given time.

"You know, I've been wondering why you let her do that," one of the other analysts, Angel, says. "You never would've let Rosa get away with it. Or any of us for that matter."

"And I don't remember asking your opinion," I snap, leveling the smarmy looking guy with my gaze. "I also didn't allow the analyst before you question the way I choose to run my staff either. So do you *really* want me to answer that?"

He mutters something about my choices being great the way they are, then excuses himself to get a round of drinks. Unsurprisingly, the rest of the team offers to help him, leaving me on my own just as Becca reaches me. I almost groan when her scent touches my nose. There's something so sweet and familiar about it, almost . . . innocent too.

"Wow. And here I was thinking they liked me," she says, sliding her hands into her skirt pockets and offering a self-deprecating smile. "Maybe I smell. Do I smell bad?" No. You smell like cookie dough and warm Sunday mornings, and if someone bottled that scent and pitched it to me I'd throw everything I had at it just to keep it *off* the market. I don't want her scent on anyone else's body.

"I sent them away."

"Oh." She frowns then rubs her lips together before meeting my eyes again. "Is it because I shouldn't be here? Is this some analysts only thing? Because I can leave. I'm not here to—"

"No." For some reason my hand shoots out and wraps around her upper arm when she moves to step away. "Stay."

She stops, but I don't miss the way she sucks in her breath and holds it, her cheeks turning bright pink as she looks up at me, her lips parted. "OK. I can stay a while."

With a slow inhale, I relax my hand and let her go.

"Let me at least buy you a drink." I lift the same hand that gripped her into the air to signal a waitress.

"I'd like that. Thanks."

"Hey, Mr. Kennedy. What'll it be?" a waitress asks, quickly appearing by my side—perk of being the owner's best friend.

"Lady's choice," I say, sliding my still-tingling hand into my pocket before I do something stupid and try to touch her again.

"My choice?" Becca's delicate brow creases as she thinks. "Yikes. I'm not really much of a drinker. What would you recommend?" She turns expectantly to the waitress.

"Oh, I'm a big fan of the cocktails here," the waitress says. "Strawberry daiquiri or cosmopolitan tastes the best."

Becca's lips form an O shape as her eyes widen. "I like strawberry."

"And she said she's not much of a drinker," I say as I place my hand on the waitress's order pad to stop her from writing. "She'll be legless in half an hour drinking something like that. Get her a Blushing Rose."

The waitress's eyes swing to Becca's. "Are you fine with him ordering for you?" I struggle to hide my smirk, but I do like seeing women looking out for each other in this world. And normally, I'd say I'm not a risky guy to be around, but where Rebecca Maxwell is concerned, I don't think I can be trusted.

Becca grins as her eyes swing back to mine. "Since

he's paying and I'm the gatekeeper of his time, I don't think he'd choose something I'll hate." *Is that a threat?* She smirks at me and, oh my God, I want to pull her hair and smack her ass for being cheeky like that.

"You heard the lady," I say instead, noting the hoarseness in my voice. When the waitress jots down the order and leaves, I turn my attention back to Becca and quirk my brow. "The gatekeeper of my time?"

"Those are your words," she says with a slight tilt of her head. "I'm just repeating them with a little flair."

"OK," I say, looking away because if I keep looking at her I'm likely to wrap an arm possessively around her. This is why I don't interact with her at the office. Time isn't making this attraction lessen. In fact, I want her more now than I did in the beginning. And what's worse, is that now she's settled into the job, there's no way in hell I can fire her. She's the best executive assistant I've ever had. No one can do her job the way she can. Hell, no one can make the team perform as well as she can either. She's better than me in every way and I love it.

"This is nice," she says suddenly. "We don't talk much in the office, so it's nice to see you acting . . . human."

"I'll try and take that as a compliment."

"It wasn't," she says with a smirk. "What's in this blushing rose drink, anyway?"

I have to blink to clear my thoughts away before I can respond to her. "Ah . . . citrus liqueur, pomegranate juice, and rose nectar. It'll be refreshing without knocking you on your ass."

"Sounds delicious. You obviously know your cocktails."

I meet her eyes, and I can't help the way my mouth kicks up at the corners. "I know a lot of things, Rebecca," I state, downing the last of my drink and wishing I'd ordered another for me too. Becca blushes at my words, and damn if I don't get a kick out of doing that to her.

"Becca! What on earth brought you down here?" Scott asks, completely interrupting the moment as he appears at my side.

"I hear this is the place to be if you work on Wall Street," she says, looking up at the tall but skinny man that is Scott Treville.

"Sure is. I wasn't sure what you drink, so I got you this." He hands her a glass of white wine which she accepts with a grateful smile. I hold back a growl. God, I hate seeing her smile at anyone but me—even though I go out of my way to make it so she *doesn't* smile at me.

"Grabbed one for you too, boss," he adds, handing me my usual vodka lime, which earns him a couple of brownie points and lessens my need to mark a territory that isn't even mine.

"Thanks," I say, taking it just as the waitress arrives with the drink I bought for Becca on a tray.

"Blushing Rose," she says, smiling as she offers it to Becca, who has an obvious moment of not knowing what to do when presented with two drinks at once. So, I help her out in the decision-making process by taking the wine from her hand, swapping it with the low-proof cocktail and telling the waitress she can take the wine away.

Scott clears his throat beside me but ignores the obvious posturing on my part. "OK then. Do you want me to show you around, Bec? Introduce you to a few people?"

Bec. Since when did he earn the right to shorten her name further than it already was?

Becca opens her mouth, but once again I answer for her. "She's fine here with me." My jaw tenses as I meet Scott's beady eyes. I really shouldn't call them beady because they're not, but coming over here and sleazing on my girl right in front of me makes him a weasel. Wait. What the fuck am I doing? She is not and never has been my girl. Nor will she ever be. I'm her boss. The company forbids inter-office relationships and I'm being fucking stupid.

"Oh, uh . . . OK then." Scott steps away, but I'm quick to snap myself out of whatever the bullshit is that's going on inside my head.

"Wait," I say, hating myself for acting this way—showing weakness and indecisiveness—in front of an employee, needing to force my words through my teeth. "I have something to attend to. So, if you *could* show her around, introduce her to a few people, maybe, then I think that'd help out the team." I pause and look between the both of them, my eyes landing on Scott's as I drive a final point home. "Just remember our company has a no fraternization policy. This is work only."

Scott baulks immediately. "What? No. That was—"

"Nooooo," Becca says, shaking her head emphatically. "We're definitely not— This isn't . . . It was never going to . . . I'm here for . . ." She stops and clears her throat. "We're just friends."

Scott nods. "Definitely just friends. Becca and I bat for different teams."

I look between them, their awkward denial somehow making me feel a hell of a lot better leaving Becca in Scott's care. *Maybe I'll keep him on the team a little longer.*

"OK," I say, downing the last of my drink then excusing myself.

"Thanks for the drink," Becca calls after me. "And the, er, company. It was a nice change of pace."

"Sure," I say before turning around and getting as far away from Becca as possible. My skin feels hot and my dick feels like the needle on a compass, urging me to point back toward her. I really need to quit lusting after a girl I can't have. This is getting ridiculous.

BECCA

"Well, he was pleasant as always," Scott says with a forced smile as Ronan disappears into the crowd.

"So it isn't just me then?" I ask, looking around the artfully designed bar and finding great delight in how everything is bank related. There's a ticket machine that calls you up to a teller-style bar among other things. At the same time, I'm trying to find Peter and his team, although I wish he'd made it clear this afternoon that my team would also be here. It seems in poor taste to ask me here when he's also trying to poach me from Ronan. What if I'd already been here with Pete when Ronan arrived? That would have looked terrible and possibly made for an even worse working relationship than we already have. Unless, of course, that was the point?

I press my lips together, suddenly very annoyed with my brother.

"—mingle and try to listen in on anything interesting. It's pretty much all anyone is here to do," Scott says, obviously giving me the rundown of the Wall St etiquette at Banked Up, and I've barely caught a word.

"I'm so sorry, I couldn't quite hear you over the din," I say, telling a half-truth. "But what you're basically saying is that this is where everyone mingles and talks business? It's not all technical research."

"Exactly," he says with a smile. "You catch on quick. I don't know why they kept you in admin so long."

"Probably because I do the work of about three people in a day," I state, taking a sip of my drink and feeling surprised that it tastes exactly the way Ronan described.

"I see the Jerk of Wall Street has run off to speak to people more on his level," Katerina, one of only two female analysts on our team says as she arrives with the rest of the team.

"I think I frightened him away," I joke, catching his eye from where he talks with a group across the room. I look away quickly, my heart kicking up a beat.

"What do you have over that guy, anyway?"

"Why would I have something over him?"

"Well, you know? The whole knitting thing really has us all perplexed."

"So, you think I'm blackmailing Ronan into paying me to knit?"

"It's either that, or you're sleeping with the guy. But with the dowdy way you dress, no one is thinking that."

She lets out a trill laugh as I run my hand down the front of my skirt, wondering what my outfit has to do with anything. It's corporate attire. It's just not identical to what everyone else wears to the office.

"What's wrong with my clothes?" I ask, looking from her to Scott who opens his mouth to answer moments before a gruff voice cuts in.

"Absolutely nothing," Ronan growls, placing a hand on the small of my back to guide me away. "I thought I told you to show her around." That last part is aimed at Scott, whose mouth is now flapping without words.

"I...I..."

Ronan turns his attention to Katerina who's shrunk back, looking mortified over getting caught with her claws out. "I think you'll find that Bec is just so fucking good at her job that she has time to knit. You could take lessons, Katerina."

Katerina's mouth opens just as we turn away, and I can't ignore the tiny thrill I get from seeing the put-together blonde get knocked on her ass in my honor.

"You didn't have to do that," I say once we're far enough away from her. I can feel my cheeks flushed with heat. I never expected Ronan to have my back like that.

"Yes, I did. I won't have any of my team second guessing my intentions." He looks right past me, his jaw tight as he barks at Scott to get over here. "I'm heading off. Keep her by your side at all times. And *mingle*. You're here to network."

"Yes, sir," Scott says with a straight-backed salute. "I'm in your service."

Ronan grunts. "Don't let anyone question your place on this team again," he says to me before taking his hand from my back and turning away, practically sprinting for the door.

"What on earth just happened?" I breathe, looking from Ronan's receding back to Scott's perplexed face.

"I have *no* idea. I've never seen him like that."

"Do you think I have something on Ronan too?"

"No." He blinks and turns his attention full to me. "Anyone with half a brain knows you're the reason Ronan hasn't gone on a firing spree lately. I think the only thing you have of Ronan's is his respect…And his protection from the looks of things."

"You really think so?"

He looks at me for a moment and smiles. "I do. Forget about Kat and her claws. You've earned your place here. You just heard it from the boss himself."

"Becca! I thought that was you," a familiar voice says to my left. I turn to find my brother smiling with a drink in his hand. "What time did you get here?"

"Not that long ago," I say, catching the curious look on Scott's face. "Scott, do you know Peter Greer?"

Scott frowns as he looks from me to Peter. "Of course. He's up for senior partner along with Ronan. Question is, how do *you* know him?"

"I invited her here," Pete says before I can answer, meeting Scott's eyes in challenge. I realize I was right with my earlier summation. My brother is using me to piss Ronan off.

Well, joke's on him because Ronan isn't here anymore and I'm not going to be for long either.

"She's not a part of your team," Scott says

"Doesn't mean I can't recognize ability when I see it. It's something Ronan probably should have started nurturing months ago. He's letting her talent go to waste leaving her just sitting there in front of his office all day."

"I don't think—"

"You know what," I interject. "I think maybe that cocktail went to my head a little too much. I'm just going to head home myself."

I hear my name, but I've already started walking and I'm not going to look back. The next time my brother and I speak, we will be having words and not good ones either.

When I get outside, I hail the first cab I find instead of waiting for my driver, then I head back to my apartment, immediately texting my brother to tell him I'm not a pawn before dialing my most trusted number.

"Nina?" I say when it connects. "I need you to be really honest with me. Is there something wrong with the way I dress?"

BECCA

"I've been waiting for this day for years," Nina says, piling my arms full of clothes to try on the next day after work.

"Seriously?" I ask, my voice muffled against the fabric. "Then why didn't you say something?"

"Because you were happy with it." She turns around and meets my eyes with hers. "Just because your personal style doesn't match my personal style doesn't mean I get to dis yours."

"But now that I have asked?" I lift my brows, a smirk tilting the corner of my mouth.

"Well, that's an entirely different ball game." She breaks out into a full-on smile. "Cue the makeover montage." She swipes her hand upward and clicks in the air. And I wish that this shopping expedition could be summed up in a simple musical montage. Because getting my body in and out of several different suits, blouses, and heels—not to mention the accessories she insisted I needed with each outfit—took hours. By the time we finished and I had an entire wardrobe full of upgraded workwear, my feet hurt and my credit card was crying under the stress. And me? I was feeling exactly like the young girl I was back in high school when I was told that the dress I wore to the homecoming dance looked like it belonged in a thrift store. And really, that's exactly where I got it from, so they weren't wrong. But I'd put a lot of effort into jazzing it up and making it my own, and I'd left the house that night feeling the prettiest I'd ever felt. All it took was a single comment from a nasty girl whose parents could afford to buy brand new clothes off the rack to derail me. Here I am over a decade later letting a pretty girl in a designer suit get under my skin to the point where I just spent a ridiculous amount of money on new clothes to prove her wrong. Some things never change.

"My dad is going to be so disappointed in me," I say as I slump on my couch and survey the overflowing bags littered about my living room.

"Disappointed? I would have thought your dad would be proud of you for everything you've accomplished." Nina slurps the last of her bubble tea from the bottom of her cup. "I mean, look at you. Look at this apartment. Look at how far you've come in just a few short months. You've seriously leveled up, girl."

"He hates flashy displays of wealth," I say, reaching into the bag beside me. I pull out a plum-colored silk blouse and run my thumb over the fabric. It feels so luxurious, and as much as I love it, there's still a little voice inside of me saying this is too much. I don't deserve this.

"Why do you think that is?" she asks.

I bounce my shoulders. "We never really had much growing up. Dad was a woodwork teacher before he retired, and he didn't make a lot. Mom used to throw herself into pyramid scheme after pyramid scheme trying to chase that next big thing that would bring in the big bucks. Dad hated her for it. He couldn't see why she wasn't happy with what we *did* have. And she hated that dad was actually happy with what *little* we had."

"Is that why they split?"

"Yeah. Part of it. I was at college for maybe a month before she took me out to lunch one day and announced she was leaving dad for some guy she met online who owns a golf course and a private jet. I have no clue what he did to earn all of that, but she's happy now in her waterfront property in the Bahamas."

"And how about your dad? Still penny pinching on Staten Island?"

"Yup. Both Peter and I have offered to help him. But he always insists he doesn't want money. He only ever wants time."

"Well, time is money."

"Yes. But you can't buy time. That's the part he always catches you on."

"I guess some people are socialists through and through and capitalism is never going to sit well with them. But that doesn't mean that you have to feel bad for participating. Didn't having the ability to go and buy all this stuff make you feel good?"

"At the time," I admit. "Definitely."

"Then what does it matter what your dad thinks? You're a grown-ass woman who can make her own choices and be comfortable thriving in this capitalist society we work in the middle of. We're on Wall Street for fuck's sake. That is literally the place where money is the only language people understand. You going to work tomorrow looking like a fine piece of ass in that new skirt suit, will make Katerina eat her words. And Ronan is going to be so impressed he's likely to bend you over his desk and have his wicked way with you." She waggles her brows, and I can't help but laugh at how preposterous that idea is.

"That is not the goal of all of this," I insist, even though the idea is like a little brain worm wiggling about inside my head whispering, *what if? What if he looks differently at you now?*

"Well, it should be," she says, glancing at her watch before she stands and picks up her coat off the arm of the couch. "You are a beautiful, intelligent, highly capable woman who deserves to land an equally beautiful, intelligent and highly capable man. Ronan Kennedy fits that bill. In fact, I hazard to say that you might just be too good for him." She gives me a wink and grabs her purse, waving over her shoulder as she heads to the front door.

With a scoff, I jump up and follow her. "You're saying all of this like you actually think I have a chance," I say as she opens the door. "The man barely even speaks to me."

"Yeah, but he hasn't fired you. And he lets you knit."

"And?"

"And you don't have anything on him."

"You're starting to sound like Katerina here."

"Just think about it," she says, resting her hand on the door handle. "Men are simple creatures and Katerina was right about one thing. If you don't have anything on him, then the only other reason he'd let you get away with knitting all afternoon is because there's something else going on."

"Wait. You don't actually . . . are you trying to tell me that you think he is interested in me?" I jab a finger at the center of my chest. "Me?"

Nina laughs. "Yeah. You."

"No."

"Yes."

"No. The knitting privileges are solely because of my work abilities."

"Sure they are," she says, starting to close the door on her way out. "See you at work, knitty-kitty." She makes a purring sound and then suddenly the door clicks shut and I'm on my own, scoffing and shaking my head because the idea that Ronan could have any interest in me is ridiculous. In three months he's barely said three words to me. And the only nice thing he's done for me is not fire me. Oh, and buy me a drink at Banked Up. Other than that, I doubt I'm even a blip on his radar. I bought all of these new clothes to prove Katerina wrong and show her that I can be just as beautiful and put together as any other woman at Pierce Goodman. But now I have a second thing to prove too—no matter how well dressed and put together I am, my position and privileges were completely earned. Ronan Kennedy has zero interest in my round ass. I'm just not in that man's league, despite what Nina says.

RONAN

The clack of heels outside my office door precedes a flurry of conversation that pulls me from the mass of emails I'm trying to work through.

"Rebecca," I call out, pressing my fingers to the bridge of my nose as I try to fight the headache brewing at the top of my skull. I've barely slept a wink since Banked Up, filthy dreams of Rebecca keeping me restless and dashing to the bathroom before I destroy my sheets. *This is getting out of hand.*

"Yes, Ronan?" The clacking gets closer. And when I look up, my jaw about hits the floor. "Is something wrong?"

"What . . ." My eyes move from her face to her feet and then back up again. My cock joins in and reacts in its own way. "What happened to your regular clothes?"

She looks down as if seeing the figure accentuating suit, blouse, and heels for the first time. "A friend of mine knows how to shop. She took me somewhere that does corporate for curves. I was tired of looking so dowdy all the time." She looked perfect all the time to me.

"And this is what the commotion out there is about?" Why is my throat so dry?

"Ah . . . yeah. Caused a bit of a stir among the team. But I'll tell them to keep it down so you can get on with your work."

"Thank you," I say, taking a sip of my coffee as I try to work through what my reaction to her truly is. She's stunning no matter what she wears, and while this skirt suit makes her look both gorgeous and professional, I can't help but miss the sweater vests and pleated skirts. I don't know what it was about them that I liked. Maybe it was that they were different to what everyone else on this floor wears and felt novel. Or maybe it was just because they were so . . . her.

"Will that be all?"

"Ah . . . yeah. Thank you."

She nods. "No problem."

"And, Rebecca?"

"Yes?"

"You look good no matter what you wear."

Heat rises in her cheeks as she presses her lips together then nods. "Careful, Ronan. I might start to think you like me if you say anything too kind."

Her words cause me to laugh as she steps out the door, pulling it shut behind her and cutting her from my view. Which is just as well, because I only would have stared at her ass as she sauntered back toward her desk, this new skirt giving me a clear indication as to where all of her curves start and finish.

It's then that it hits me what I liked about her old clothes. It was the secrets lying within. They gave me just a hint of her shape, and although I knew there'd be peaks and valleys of soft flesh underneath, I needed my imagination to work out exactly where they were. But now, with the waist cinched and the skirt fitted, I don't have to close my eyes and imagine. I can just see.

With my eyes open, she's *all* that I can see now. And *that* is a problem.

Three months. Three months she's worked for me, and for three months, I've had to fight my focus. I'd thought that keeping her on staff would mean that I'd grow accustomed to having her around and this obscene attraction of mine would fizzle away to admiration and then to the mild annoyance I have around the majority of humans in this world. But with Becca, my attraction has remained, with admiration and respect joining it in a group huddle.

After the first month, I'd thought that her comment regarding her slimy landlord was the reason I was always wondering where she was outside of work hours—so I found her an apartment in a secure building and provided a car service to keep her from walking alone on the street. But that didn't work. Now that I knew exactly where she lived, I thought about her even more.

Then, I thought that maybe I was still in lust with

her because she was the first assistant I'd had who actually managed to get through her work without royally fucking up five times a day. So, I started telling the analysts to run all of their research through her before it came to me. I was expecting the extra work to show some sort of cracks. But come lunchtime, she was still sitting there knitting away with nothing left do. And I had a team of analysts who were performing better than ever. I didn't just lust after her at this point, I'd begun to respect her too.

Day after day, we followed the same ritual. And day after day, my feelings toward her grew. Comments were made about the knitting from my colleagues and higher ups, but when my numbers had me at the pinnacle of the game, they couldn't deny that what I was doing was working. So no matter how 'unprofessional' the knitting looked, I wasn't willing to make it stop. If I had my way, I could listen to the sound twenty-four, seven. It's always been a sound of comfort to me.

Angel asked me at Banked Up what she has over me for me to let her get away with knitting on the job, and while I couldn't admit it then, I can admit it to myself. She has my heart. I'm one hundred percent infatuated with the woman who gatekeeps my time. And if I could choose to spend it as I wanted, I'd spend it all with her, sitting in front of a fire, listening to the sound of her needles. *Click-clack, click-clack.*

A knock at the door pulls me from my thoughts, Scott's head poking not a moment later.

"Do we have a meeting?" I ask, scowling at the interruption.

"Ahh, no. But I felt that I needed to speak to you about something," he says, stepping in a little further and closing the door behind him. "Something private."

"Private how?" I ask, the little hairs on the back of my neck standing up.

"It's about . . . " He pauses and pulls slightly at his necktie.

"Spit it out, kid," I snap, hating any sort of indecisiveness.

"Becca. It's about Becca."

"What about her?"

"I don't really know how to say this, and I've sat with it for a full day and I still don't know, so I'll just come out with it. At Banked Up, after you left, Peter Greer turned up."

"What did he want?"

"Her. He said he was the one who invited her."

"What? Why?"

"I think . . . I think he wants to poach her from our team."

I slam my hands on my desk and shoot to my feet. "Mother fucker!"

BECCA

Ronan's voice rises and falls, and I wonder what on earth Scott said to him that has him so outrageously angry. It's been weeks since I've heard Ronan go off like this, and as far as I know, Scott wasn't working on a project that could illicit this kind of a response. But he did say that he had something important to speak to him about before the pitch meetings start today, and when Scott practically rushes out of Ronan's office with his tail between his legs, I'm left here wondering if maybe . . . maybe this outburst has something to do with me.

"Rebecca." Ronan's voice calling from within his office has my spine straightening as dread fills my belly.

"What did you say?" I hiss at Scott.

"I told him about Greer."

Heat climbs up my neck. "You didn't? Oh my god, Scott. You have no idea what you're doing."

"So, he isn't trying to poach you from our team?"

"I . . . he . . . Yes. But, Jesus. I wasn't leaving."

"Rebecca." Ronan's tone is more insistent now.

"Then you'd better convince him of that."

"I thought we were friends," I scowl, getting out of my seat to go and face the music.

"We are. Which is why I'm making sure that scumbag stays far away from you."

My brow pinches. "Scumbag? Are you talking about Peter?"

"*Rebecca.*"

I jolt slightly and shoot Scott a look of hurt confusion as I move toward Ronan's office. I can't believe he took word of that ridiculous conversation at Banked Up to Ronan. The fact I walked away should have been enough for both Pete and Scott to know I didn't want any part of it.

"Yes, Ronan," I say calmly, my palms sweating as I stand across from his desk.

"Take a seat."

"I'd rather stand."

"Fine." He places the pen in his hand on his desk then stands, his tall frame elegantly unfolding until he's walking around the desk to stand in front of me. "We'll stand then."

My eyes travel from his feet to his face, taking in the narrow hips and the broad shoulders, dressed perfectly as always in a tailored suit and a white button-up shirt and tie. If Harvey Spector and Mike Ross had a love child, that child could be Ronan Kennedy. He has the looks, the smarts, the arrogance, *and* the good dress sense.

"Is this where you fire me?"

"On what grounds would I do that?" He folds his arms across his middle, his blue eyes boring into mine.

"I'm not going to give you something. If you wanna get rid of me, you'll need to do that yourself."

"I'm not interested in getting rid of you, Rebecca," he says, softening his tone and relaxing his stance. "What did Greer offer you?"

"Nothing that I accepted."

"What did he offer?"

Releasing a sigh, it's me who folds my arms across my middle this time. "The chance to learn under him and triple what I make right now."

"You want to learn to do what I do?"

"For the record, I didn't approach him about this. He offered and I refused."

"But are you interested in learning everything about venture capital or not?"

"I'm interested," I admit. "But I think I'm learning plenty where I am."

"Any complaints?"

"There's just not enough to keep me busy. There's only so much knitting a girl can do before she gets restless."

He sucks in a breath slightly at that, and I wonder what for. Surely it wasn't a response to my feelings toward my knitting?

"OK," he says after a moment's deliberation. "You can go."

He waves me off and I turn immediately, stopping only when he calls out to me. "And cancel my meetings for the rest of the day, please. I have some . . . thinking to do."

"Are you going to fire me?" I ask, fearing not only for my paycheck but for my apartment too. I don't think I could afford it on my own, which would mean I'd be forced to work for Pete, and I don't want to do that because I'm mad at my brother right now. He's stirred up some shit he had no right stirring.

"I don't know what I'm going to do just yet. Peter Greer and I have a longstanding rivalry. I don't like that you were talking to him behind my back. I also don't like that he's trying to steal my best team member from under me."

"I wasn't aware you two weren't on good terms. But for the record, the only reason I was talking to him was—"

"I'm not interested in the why, Rebecca. I'm only interested in what comes next. Something I can decide if you'd cancel my meetings like I asked."

"Of course," I whisper, pressing my teeth into my cheek as I walk out of his office and pull the door closed behind me.

"What'd he say?" Scott asks as soon as I'm back at my desk.

I shoot him an unimpressed glare. "He needs time to think."

"He won't fire you," he says when I make it obvious I don't want to talk. "You're too good."

"I just don't understand why you did this."

"Greer doesn't deserve you."

"And Ronan does?"

"I don't know. But I at least feel like I do. We're a *team,* Bec. You shouldn't even be thinking about jumping ship." The hurt look in his eyes pulls at my heartstrings, and the vast majority of my anger dissipates.

"I was never going to leave the team, Scott. Peter was trying to convince me to, yes. But I'd already told him no."

"Then why were you at Banked Up to meet him?"

"I don't know." I release a sigh. "Because he *asked* me. And because . . . he's going to kill me for telling you this, but he's the one who caused this problem in the first place."

"Oh my god. What?" he blurts before I can continue.

"He's my big brother."

Scott's eyes go wide and he steps back like my admission made him stumble. "What?"

"He's my brother."

"I heard that. But how? You have different names and you're not married, right?"

"I use our mother's name in the office. It was to keep us separate so I could work my way up without it looking like I was getting favoritism. But all that went out the window the moment Peter tried to use our relationship to stir up whatever this is with Ronan. I'm so mad at him right now."

"I'm reeling here. I can't believe that you are related to that man. It feels impossible. Were you raised in the same house?"

"Yes," I say, a sudden laugh bursting out of me.

"Are you sure? Or was it a Harry Potter type situation where they made you live in a cupboard under the stairs and he threw tantrums over how many presents he got for his birthday each year?"

"What? No. We were treated the same way. He's just more like my mom. And I take after my dad. They were very different people."

"Oh no. Your mom's one of those mega-bitches, isn't she? You poor thing."

"She wasn't. She was fine. She just . . . had different priorities and . . . oh my god, why am I telling you this stuff. I'm mad at you too."

"For loving you enough to risk our friendship by making sure Ronan does whatever it takes to keep you on team Kennedy?"

I open my mouth to retaliate but then I just close it again, because when he puts it like that, it kind of knocks the wind right out of my sails. "Well, I'm trying to be angry at you. We'll see what Ronan does before I call it though."

"Hey, as long as we're still working together tomorrow morning, then I'm a happy guy."

The last of my resolve melts as I look down and smile. "You know, it's kind of nice to feel this wanted. I don't think I've ever had anyone fight like this for me before. But then, I've never worked this hard before either. Being transferred up here really lit a firecracker under my ass. I was so petrified of getting fired that I haven't been late to work once."

"Ronan has that effect on people. And you, my dear friend, have the ability to do the one thing he—brilliant as he is—couldn't."

"What's that?"

"You got us all working together as a team."

Pride blooms in the center of my chest as the compliment sinks in. "Yeah. I guess I kind of did. Not too bad for some random admin girl, huh?"

"Random?" Scott frowns. "There was nothing random about you getting this promotion, Bec. You were recommended."

"What? By whom?"

RONAN

"What do you plan to do?" Banks asks on the other end of the line as I sit back in my chair, staring out the wall of windows and over the city streets below.

"What I want to do is punch that scheming fucker in the face and teach him a lesson for trying to go behind my back."

"I get it. But that isn't how Gran raised us, right? How do you win without throwing down?"

"I'm having a hard time thinking of anything besides wringing his neck." Releasing a harsh breath, I scrape my hand over my face and stand, deciding pacing the room will serve me better instead.

"Keep thinking then. We've known Peter Greer long enough to know that he'll do whatever it takes to get the better of you. How do you get the better of him?"

"I beat him at his own game."

"And what game is that?"

"He's rattling cages, trying to find a weakness in my team."

"How do you stop him from doing that?"

"Match his offer. But if he tries this on all of my team members, I'll burn through my budget."

"OK. That's a start. But it sounds unsustainable. What is?"

"Keeping him away from my team entirely. But to do that, I'd have to—" I stop abruptly, knowing where Banks is trying to steer me because he's been doing this for a while now. "I'd have to start my own Venture Capital firm and get whoever is willing to follow to sign non-competes."

"It's the only way you'll have the career you want, my friend," he says, and I know deep down that he's right.

"What if I don't have what it takes to do this on my own?" I say, voicing my innermost fears and the reason I've waited so long to do this.

"You do," he insists. "I know you, man. You've got this. And you know I'm always gonna be here to bounce any ideas off of. I've been right where you are, wondering where to next, and I already walked my path. How about you let me help you walk yours?"

"Like as a partner?" The weight of this decision suddenly feels about a ton lighter at the prospect.

"I was meaning as a friend with advice."

"No. I think it should be as a partner. Just think

about it, Banks. You and me doing business. We've always worked well together, and we both excel at crisis management. Just look at what we did to bring down those assholes at Wright Media last year. We put our heads together and got Isla the position that was rightfully hers."

"I know, man, and it was a rush. But between the bar and spending time with Isla, I don't think I'll have time to work on this with you."

"What if you were more of a consultant? Or even a *silent* partner. You'll basically be making money for nothing since I call you to talk out all my problems anyway."

Banks chuckles down the line. "OK. If I say yes, will you leave that fucking company and do this?"

"With my brother from another mother on my side? Abso-fucking-lutely."

"I'm probably insane for considering this, but why the hell not. You have yourself a partner, Ronan. Well, a silent one, anyway."

"We're doing this?"

"Yeah. We are."

"OK. Now we need to talk strategy. I have to figure out how I can leave this place, get as much of my team as possible to jump ship with me *and* retain as many clients as I can before the higher ups realize what I'm doing."

"It's not gonna be easy. But since we single-handedly pulled apart Wright Media, I have a feeling we're the best men for the job," Banks says as I drop my weight back into my chair then pick up my pen.

"First thing's first—where the hell are we even gonna operate from?"

"Now *that* I can help you with."

BECCA

"Can you gather the team in the meeting room in thirty minutes, please?" Ronan says via the internal line. It's the first bit of communication I've had with him since he locked himself in there earlier, and the simple request has my heart hammering against my rib cage. What is this about?

"Of course. Will they need to bring anything with them?"

"No. Just themselves. Thirty minutes." He disconnects.

I stare at the silent receiver for about ten seconds before I glance up and find Scott staring right at me from his desk, a look that says, 'well?' on his face.

Hitting the number for *his* internal line, I gesture to his desk phone as it starts to ring.

"What'd he say?"

"He wants us in the meeting room in thirty minutes."

"Us? As in you and me?"

"No. The whole team."

"Really? Shit. I wonder what his plan is."

"Maybe he's just going to ignore it and pretend nothing happened?" I suggest.

"No." I can see Scott shake his head and purse his lips in thought. "That's not Ronan's MO. He's definitely going to retaliate in some way. The question is how?"

"I guess we'll find out in half an hour."

"I'll help wrangle the troops."

"Thanks, Scott."

We disconnect, and I log out of my computer before standing from my desk, ready to head into the break room where I already know Katerina and Angel just went. The moment I round the corner, I almost run smack bam into Peter. He catches me by the arms and laughs it off like he hasn't just caused a shit storm in my team with his games.

"Becca! I was just on my way to see you. You left Banked Up in such a rush that I never got to introduce you to my team members. We can do it now if you like."

"I'm quite certain that the text I sent following my departure made it clear to you that I'm not especially happy with you right now, Peter."

"I'm not trying to use you as a pawn," he says, sliding his hands in his pockets and rocking on his heels. "I'm offering you an opportunity. You've more than proven your capabilities on Ronan's team, and I already have the approval to get you the salary we discussed."

"Except we didn't discuss anything, Pete. You're just railroading me and expecting me to do whatever you tell me. I don't know if you remember this from our arguments as kids, but you're not the boss of me."

"Something I'm trying to change," he says with a smirk.

"You're annoying me."

"You're annoying *me*. Just take the offer and we'll call it a day."

"God. Quit being so pushy. I said no. You are such a spoiled brat!"

I push past him and just like he did when we'd fight as kids, he leans in and says, "Takes one to know one."

Being the mature young woman that I am, I poke my tongue out at him, earning myself a deep belly laugh as he saunters away. As soon as I'm in the break room, I find Katerina and Angel staring at me.

"What's with you and the partners in this place?" Katerina asks, looking to the doorway Peter just vacated.

I grab a mug and busy myself making tea. "What do you mean?"

"Peter Greer is chasing you around like you're some hot commodity, and Ronan just lets you do whatever you want. What are you? The CEOs daughter or something?"

"What if she's, like, an undercover boss?" Angel suggests.

Katerina's eyes go wide. "You're right. What if she *is* the boss?"

They both look to me with questions in their eyes

while I just roll mine and sigh. "I'm not anyone's boss. But speaking of bosses, Ronan wants us all in the meeting room in about"—I check my watch—"twenty minutes."

"What for? I thought he cancelled the pitch meeting for today."

"I don't know what he wants to talk about, but I do know it's not a pitch meeting. I'll see you in there." Carrying my mug full of steaming tea out of the room, I ignore the murmurs behind me and focus on making sure everyone is ready and available before Ronan is. We all make it into our seats about twenty seconds before the man walks in, an air of tension about him as he moves to stand at the top of the table.

"Thank you all for coming," he says, looking around the table slowly and finishing with his eyes on me. "I've been doing a bit of soul searching today."

Something about the warmth in his eyes makes my breathing quicken. I have to look down and away before I make my crush on him obvious to the entire room.

Ronan returns to addressing the room as a whole. "I've made a decision that will not only affect my future, but also the future of each and every one of you at this table." He pauses for effect then continues. "I've decided that it's time for me and Pierce Goodman to part ways."

My hand flies to my chest as I suck in a breath, and I'm not the only one. Seems audible gasps are catching in this room.

"What does that mean for us?" Katerina asks immediately.

"That's what I'm in here to discuss with you. I plan to open my own venture capital firm, so those of you willing to jump ship with me are welcome aboard. I chose you all very specifically, and as the very first team in the door, you'll all benefit from shares in the company as part of your signing package."

"Will you be matching our current salary and benefits package?" Angel asks, exchanging glances with others who nod in agreement with his question.

"That's something I'll need to discuss with you all on an individual basis. I'm not Pierce Goodman, but I do aim to be their rival, and I think that with my track record, and your help, we can do that."

"And what happens if we don't join you?" Angel says, obviously the spokesperson of the team now.

"I don't know," Ronan says with a shrug. "They'll either replace me, add you to other partner's teams or they'll let you go."

A murmur moves about the room and it's Katerina's voice that rises above it. "How long do we have to decide this?"

Ronan looks at his watch. "About five minutes, I'd guess. Because the moment the higher ups read my resignation email, I'll be escorted out of the building and I won't get the chance to talk to you again."

A commotion outside the meeting room tells us we have even less time than that, and a wave of panicked voices erupts, questions about trust, security, health insurance, benefits, and location ensues.

"They're coming," Ronan says, glancing out the frost glass paneling to where building security is fast approaching. "I know this is a risk, but you all need to make your choice."

"Captain my captain!" Scott shoots out of his chair and salutes.

"I'm taking that as a yes?" Ronan says, a single perfect brow raised.

Scott nods. "You had me at hello."

With a slight chuckle, Ronan turns his attention to me. "What about you, cashmere? You with me?"

"I . . ." I open my mouth, a tightness in my chest making it hard for me to jump in with an answer. In my head, there are two competing voices, one telling me I'd be crazy to give up my salary and my apartment on a whim and a hope that this man will lead me to something better, and the other telling me that money isn't all there is and it's better to choose excitement over safety. I recognize those voices as my parents. But what is it that I want?

"Becca," Scott prods. I look from him back to Ronan.

"Please," Ronan says, his blue eyes full of need and hope as the door bursts open and security storms in.

It's the please that does it.

"I'm in," I say, shooting out of my chair just as the guard wraps a hand around Ronan's arm.

"Mr. Kennedy, we need to escort you off the premises." Ronan's answering smile is brilliant and wide, and what makes it even better is that it's directed at me.

"Thank you," he murmurs, making me nod as he's escorted toward the door.

"Us too!" Scott singsongs. "We also quit." The second guard flanks us and Scott links arms with me while we're given a moment to collect our personal belongings before we're guided toward the elevator.

On the ride down, we stand in muted pride, hopeful that this gamble pays off. But even if it doesn't, I'll be glad I took this chance, because for once in my life, I listened to my heart instead of my head. And my heart seems to be very clear—follow Ronan. Follow Ronan anywhere.

BECCA

"Welcome," a well-dressed man I've never met before says from outside at the bar, Banked Up, we visited recently. And I wonder why we're instantly returning to the scene of the crime that set off this chain of events. "I didn't have a lot of time to prepare, so you have barstools and a kitchen counter to work from today. We can do something about decking it out properly in the coming days."

He pushes open a small door that leads to a set of stairs alongside the main entrance of the bar. As we pass him, he smiles warmly, his dark eyes crinkling at the sides in a way that tells me he's close in age to Ronan.

"Just three?" he asks. The comment isn't directed at me, but I overhear it when it's said to Ronan who's coming up the stairs behind me.

"Three of us is more than enough," Ronan replies,

and I gather from the silence that this other man is accepting of that.

Once we get to the top of the stairs, there's a small landing with a door that leads into what would normally be a very beautiful apartment but is currently being used for storage. There are boxes and random pieces of equipment that belong to the bar below filling the space. The man who led us up here takes us into the well-appointed kitchen—and the only cleared out room—before he stops and turns to face us.

"OK. I thought there'd be a couple more of you, but a small team to start off with is probably for the best," he says. "Those of you who don't know me, my name is Banks Johnson. Ronan and I grew up together. We also went to college together and worked on Wall Street together for a time. I left about a decade ago and now I own the bar downstairs that you all enjoy frequenting. Except you"—his eyes land on me—"I don't think I've seen you before."

"She's Rebecca. The assistant I told you about," Ronan interjects before I have a chance to answer for myself.

"Oh." Banks's expression shifts from one of curiosity to acknowledgement, and I wonder what on earth Ronan has been saying about me. I glance his way, but his eyes have drifted to his feet. "OK. So we have an assistant, an analyst, a managing partner and a silent partner." He points to himself last. "That's not too bad . . . as long as we get started right now." He gestures to the island countertop that has several new laptops sitting in the center of it.

Ronan immediately pulls out one of the bar stools and grabs a computer, typing furiously before asking Banks if these are connected to a printer.

"The one in the bar, yes."

Ronan hits a couple more keys, and then Banks heads down to the bar to get whatever is getting printed off. That leaves us on our own for a moment, the reality of our new situation slowly sinking in.

"I know this isn't what either of you were probably expecting," Ronan says suddenly, his chin resting on top of clasped hands. "It certainly wasn't what I thought I'd be doing when I woke up this morning." He chuckles slightly and shakes his head. "I must be crazy. And you two . . ." He lifts his eyes and looks between me and Scott. "You two must be certifiable. I know we're in the business of risk. But this . . ." He shakes his head again. "I could fail. I could lose everything. And I could very well take you both down with me."

"That's an excellent pep-talk, boss," Scott says, a derisive chuckle following.

"Precisely why this was a fucked-up idea." Ronan lifts his eyes and it's the first time I've seen this unflappable man look even remotely flapped.

My heart goes out to him immediately and I step forward, placing my hand on his forearm and giving it a squeeze. "I have never met a person more focused and driven than you are, Ronan," I start. "There's a reason people jump whenever you ask them to, and it's not because they're scared of you. It's because they want to *be* you. You are brilliant at what you do. So, if anyone can pull this off it's definitely you."

"Is that why only two people on an eight-person team decided to join me?"

"Oh no, Ronan. That's not why. The rest of the team didn't come simply because they were afraid. They will never be brave enough to walk away and start again. And that is precisely why they will never be you." My thumb moves against the steely skin of his muscular forearm, and we stare at each other for a moment as the words I spoke sink in and shift something between us. It's as if he's looking at me for the first time, and honestly, I have a bit of trouble breathing from the intensity of it. It's as if the entire world around us has fallen away and all that there is, is me holding him up and him needing me to.

But as fast as that moment appears, it also dissipates, his expression shifting and that mask of professionalism slotting back into place once more. "Thank you, Rebecca," he says, clearing his throat before his eyes drop down to where I'm touching him—well, *caressing him*—and then return to mine.

"Shit. Sorry!" I snatch my hand back immediately, my cheeks heating as I realize what an inappropriately intimate thing that was to do—even if your boss is incredibly dreamy.

"It's fine," Ronan says, his attention returning to the laptop in front of him. I glance over my shoulder to Scott who looks like he's trying desperately not to laugh, and now I'm just hoping for an asteroid to hit the earth or something so the hideous embarrassment I'm feeling can end quickly.

Thankfully, Banks returns with the printed pages and I have a moment where I can turn away and cover my face with my hands.

"And here I was thinking I was the Renee Zellweger in this version of Jerry Maguire," Scott says under his breath as Banks and Ronan talk.

"What do you mean?"

Scott smirks and leans in a little closer so only I can hear him. "The unrequited affection? I thought I was the only one, but it turns out our quiet little assistant has a thing for the boss too. Not that I have a chance in hell since he's as straight as they come. But I do enjoy being around the man enough to admire him from afar."

"It's not like that," I say under my breath. "I mean, he's good looking, yeah. But that's not why I'm here."

"Sure," Scott says, giving me a wink. "Me either."

It's at that point that Banks approaches both of us with some of the printed pages in hand. He splits them in half and offers them to the both of us. "Today will be all about porting over as many clients as we possibly can before the company can call them and lock them into longer contracts or undermine their trust in Ronan. This is a race, not a leisurely walk in the park. This needs to be done as fast and as efficiently as possible."

"Got it," I say, taking the paper that's offered to me while Scott does the same.

"I'll be with Ronan if you need anything like passwords or something. Just let me know." Banks then gives us a nod and walks away, leaving Scott and I alone to do the work.

"And now comes the part where we shout 'show me the money' to get just one shitty client on board," Scott jests as he takes a seat at the counter. He pulls out his cell and starts typing in the first phone number. "Ready to prove how amazing you are?"

I take my seat, angling my chair so I can keep an eye on what Ronan and Banks are doing while still working myself. "Let's do it."

RONAN

By the end of the day, we have a handful of clients willing to leave Pierce Goodman to work exclusively with me, and we also have some pitches lined up thanks to some of Banks's and my old contacts. Pierce Goodman had worked pretty fast to get word out that I wasn't working for them anymore, so really it was only my most loyal clients willing to jump ship with me. But, it's a start. And once I start making a name for myself that's separate from Pierce Goodman, then things will surely turn around. Like Rebecca said, the other VCs on Wall Street wish they were me. All I have to do is show them why.

"I think that after this herculean effort we all deserve a drink," Banks says, cracking his neck as he rises from his seat and blows out a heavy breath. For a silent partner, he certainly put in a lot of hours for us today. And for that, I'm incredibly appreciative. With friends like him on my side I'll be unstoppable. I've got the experience and I've got the capital and I've got the support. As far as most startups go, I'm already well in the lead.

"I could probably do with a solid six drinks," I say, stretching my arms above my head and feeling the discs in my back crack and pop from the movement. "Maybe just give me the entire bottle. I sound like I'm falling apart."

"As much as I would love to drink myself to blackout status after today," Scott says as he collects his things, "I really need to get home. I have a live-in boyfriend who's going to be pissed when he finds out what I did today. So, it's best I go home and face the music sooner rather than later."

"Thank you for today, Scott," I say, standing and holding my hand out to shake his. "And thank you for taking a chance on me. It means a lot."

Scott takes my hand, shaking it as he gives me a nod. "Fastest way to make partner, am I right?"

Releasing his hand, I chuckle and step back. "Prove yourself worthy and it's yours," I say, causing Scott to do an excited little jig before he says another goodbye and heads for the door.

"I'll walk you downstairs," Banks adds, following him out and leaving Rebecca and I alone.

"What about you?" I ask as I turn her way. "You got a boyfriend who'll be mad if you stay behind for a drink?"

"No," she says, standing and grabbing her coat and bag with a sigh. "But I do have an apartment I'll need to pack up. I don't imagine they'll let me stay there long after the way we all walked out today." She touches my arm lightly as she moves past me. "So maybe we can take a raincheck on that drink?"

Without thinking, my hand shoots out and grabs hers, halting her movement. "I'm the one who got you the apartment," I blurt.

"What?" She turns to face me, and it takes a moment before I can drag my eyes up to meet hers.

"You won't have to move," I reiterate. "The company doesn't even know about the apartment. Banks and I . . . we own the whole building. It was an early investment we made as a way to give the people we cared about a better life."

"What? But . . . you said . . ." Her brow knits tight, creasing in the center as she shakes her head and swallows hard. "I don't understand."

Swiping a hand across my now stubbled jaw, I let out a sigh as I fold my arms across my chest and lean my weight against the edge of the counter. "To be honest, Rebecca. I don't really understand why I did it either. Actually, that's a lie. I do know why I did it."

"Why?" The word comes out as a whisper and I don't think she's breathing right now.

"I needed to be sure you were safe."

"Because?"

I release a chuckle, laughing uncomfortably because I know this is fucked up. Blurting this information is not the way to break it to someone. Currently, it all just sounds really fucking creepy. "Do you remember when you first came to work for me? You thought I was going to fire you on the spot, and you spoke about needing to pay rent and not wanting to deal with your scumbag landlord?"

"Vaguely."

"Well, the idea of you being in an unsafe environment made me uncomfortable, so I took steps to put you somewhere safe."

"I see," she says, playing with a loose thread on her coat that's draped over her arm. "Is that why I have the car service too? To keep me safe?"

Heat climbs up my throat as I nod. "Mm-hmm."

"And is this . . . is this something you do with all of your assistants?"

Her blue eyes meet mine and all I can do is shake my head.

"So, it's just me?"

I nod.

She swallows and steps closer to me, so close that I can feel the heat of her body as I white knuckle the edge of the countertop. "But why?"

"Because . . ." I wasn't prepared to admit to all of this today, so I'm nowhere near ready to explain my reasons or to express the fact that I can hardly stop thinking about her. She's in my dreams and all my waking thoughts, and if the only thing that comes of breaking out on my own is a chance to be with her then the risk of bankruptcy will be worth it.

"Because why?" she whispers.

My eyes drop to her mouth and the moment her tongue pokes out to wet the seam I lose all coherent thought. "Fuck," I mutter, wrapping a hand around the back of her head and slamming my mouth against hers.

She drops her coat and her bag immediately, her hands shifting to my chest as I give in to the desperate need to have her, to taste her, and when her sweet mouth opens to me on a sigh, I frame her face with both of my hands, kissing her so deep and long that I can't remember a time before her by the time I'm done.

"What the hell just happened?" she whispers in a rush when we come up for air. Her eyes are still closed and her fists are balled up against my shirt, her entire body trembling against me.

"I kissed you," I return, my voice thick and so full of want that I'm pretty sure I'm trembling too.

"Yes," she says, nodding. "I got that part. I just . . . I don't understand why."

"Open your eyes, cashmere," I murmur, my fingers sliding into her hair as she slowly flutters her lids and looks up at me. Confusion, lust, and what I think is vulnerability or hope in her gaze. "I kissed you because I couldn't *not* kiss you. It's all I've wanted to do since the first moment I saw you."

"Oh," she breathes, slowly unfurling her fists and releasing the fabric of my shirt. "OK."

"I've freaked you out, haven't I?" I say, slowly pulling away.

"No!" Her fists grab my shirt again. "I'm not freaked out. I'm just . . . surprised. I didn't even think you liked me."

"Like you? Oh, Rebecca, I more than like you. To be honest, the way my body reacts to you has been problematic these past few months."

"What?" She looks down and her cheeks color as she sees exactly what I've been dealing with. "Oh God. I had no idea."

"It's not your fault. I'm the one who doesn't have any control when it comes to you."

"I don't know if I should be flattered or be apologizing."

I reach up and brush the backs of my fingers against her soft cheek. "You have absolutely nothing to apologize for."

"In that case, would it be against company policy if I ask you to kiss me again?"

Chuckling, I shake my head. "We don't even have a company policy just yet, so I'll make sure it says that kissing is allowed."

"Consensual of course."

"Of course," I say, leaning in until my lips brush against hers. "We wouldn't want anyone abusing their power now would we?"

"Never," she whispers, her breath fanning my face seconds before I seal my mouth over hers and kiss her until neither of us needs a drink anymore.

BECCA

Flopping onto my couch, I bite the knuckle of my pointer finger to stop myself from losing it in a fit of giggles. What in the world just happened to me?

I went from being called dowdy and unattractive to making out with undoubtedly the hottest guy on Wall St within a day. It feels so surreal. I'm still processing everything that's happened.

When my phone buzzes next to me in my purse, I pull it out and find the myriad of missed calls and messages from Pete, Nina, and even Dad throughout the day. Seems word of my walk out with Ronan and Scott spread fast.

To my dad, I tap out a quick message telling him I'm fine and I'll call him tomorrow. To my brother, I simply tell him I'm still mad at being used in his games and will call *him* when I'm ready to talk. And to Nina, I hit the call button, because I *really* need some girl talk.

"Ohmigod!" Nina gasps the moment the call connects. "What the actual fuck? I've been calling you all damn day. Spill! Why were you all marched out of the building today?"

"Ronan kissed me."

"What? Is that why they made you leave? My god. The no fraternizing policy is way over the top."

"No. It wasn't before we left. It was after." I explain the drama between Peter and Ronan, the offer to have me change teams and Ronan's decision to create an entirely new company and take me and Scott with him. "I know this is a huge risk. But I feel really good about it, you know?"

"Well, of course you do," she says with a chuckle. "You have two of the most eligible bachelors in Manhattan *fighting* over you, and one of them won. The power of a new wardrobe, huh?"

"Oh God. You don't think the new wardrobe was the real reason Ronan kissed me, do you? That would be . . . shallow."

"No. Gosh no. I'm just trying to grab a little credit here for myself since I helped you pick it and the first day you wear it, all of this happens. Katerina is spitting by the way. She lusts over Peter Greer and just hates that he was interested in you over her."

"Oh yuck. Please stop insinuating that Peter is interested in me like that."

"Why on earth not. The man is *fine*."

"Ew. Stop."

"OK. So, he's no Ronan Kennedy. But how do you not see it?"

I hesitate for a moment before realizing that since I don't work for Pierce Goodman anymore, I don't have to keep it a secret. "Pete is my *brother*."

"Wait. *What?* How? You have different surnames."

"I use our mother's maiden name. It was a decision made when I was hired so he could never be accused of favoritism."

"Oh my god! Why was I never told this?"

"Because I wasn't allowed to tell anyone. HR knew. But that's it. Pete's orders."

"Jesus. I'm shook here, Bec. I don't know how I couldn't see it."

"Pete and I aren't particularly close. He's married to his job first and foremost."

"OK. Well, I'm trying not to be too offended."

"Don't be offended, Nina. Please. You're the first person I called to talk to about Ronan."

"OK," she says, and I can instantly hear the smile in her voice. "That *does* make up for it. But only if you give me more details. Like, how was the kiss? Is he the kind of guy who holds your face and kisses you with varying pressure and intensity? Because I really get that vibe off him."

With my phone pressed against my ear, I lie back on the couch and recount my day and the moment Ronan kissed me in great detail, talking until my voice turns hoarse and realizing that for the first time in my life, I have a proper best friend.

"I'm sorry I didn't confide in you about Peter," I whisper near the end of the conversation.

"That's OK," Nina whispers back. "Just don't do it again. Besties trust each other with their secrets."

"I've never had a proper best friend before."

"Well then, I'm honored to be your first."

After I hang up with Nina, I stare at the phone for a while, trying to make sense of everything that's happened. Ronan gave up his partnership at Pierce Goodman, admitted he cares about me enough to get me a safe and secure apartment then kissed me all in the same day. And while I'm touched, elated, and excited, it's all a little too much for my brain to handle. I'm buzzing.

I try to go to bed early that night, but I can't stop tossing and turning. The kiss with Ronan replays over and over in my head and I can't help but smile. He might be closing a door by leaving his job, but he's opening a new one by going out on his own. One that I can walk through with him. I still can't believe he wants me!

RONAN

It takes a few days of late nights and moving things around, but by the end of the first week Banks's old apartment no longer looks like a storage unit. It looks like a fully working office space ready to welcome clients. And thank the gods we actually have some lined up because there were a few moments on that first day where I genuinely thought I was fucked. That was nerves more than reality talking because as Banks had pointed out so many times before, I had made a name for myself in this city, and if I couldn't rely on that goodwill to get me through, then I obviously wasn't as accomplished as everyone thought. Maybe I should have listened to Banks months ago?

But then, I wouldn't have met Rebecca.

And if I had never met Rebecca, I may have never left Pierce Goodman. Because the two events are related. I left the company because I couldn't stand the idea of losing her—in a work capacity or personally. She's the most competent assistant I've ever had and she's also the first woman I've ever cared this deeply about. I know that the vast majority of the decisions I've made these past months have been about her, so I'm not going to pretend they weren't. But now, I have the opportunity to actually be with her and treat her like the queen I believe her to be. Which is why I have planned the most epic first date I can imagine. This is a culmination of the time spent fighting my attraction and realizing such a thing was futile, on top of the deep appreciation I have of her work ethic and the fact she would willingly sacrifice her job security for me.

When I look to the future she's a big part of it. I know this relationship of ours is still early days and we have to endure the stress of setting up and running a business together, but one of my highest priorities is to win her over and show her that the one and only place she belongs in this world is right by my side and in my bed. It's her for me or it's no one.

"I have Mr. Lee from the Gilchrist Confectionery Company on the line," Becca calls through from outside my new office. "Should I put him through?"

"You can. But after this, don't take any more calls. I want us to finish up for the night. Can you wait for me?"

I can hear the smile in her voice before she answers. We haven't gotten to do much more than steal a few kisses between work or over takeout this week, but I plan to make up for that tonight. "Of course," she says.

When I finish discussing the ins and outs of a global expansion plan with my client, I hang up the phone and log out of my computer, heading out of my office with a smile on my face as I go in search of Becca. She's not at her desk, which means she's probably in the kitchen area that's now set up as a break room. I head straight there and find her seated comfortably on the leather couch, the clickety clack of her knitting needles filling my chest with warmth and affection. One of the things I stipulated while setting up the office space was that she should have a comfortable place to knit when she's not busy. It's good to see her taking advantage of that.

"I probably should have had this set up in my office," I say as I move closer to her and she sets the knitting to the side. "Don't stop."

"It's a comfy couch," she says, knitting by touch as she meets my eyes and smiles. "I think it would look good in your office."

"It's not the couch I want. It's you. I like seeing you like this. The sound of it soothes me."

Her smile grows wider. "You like it when I knit?"

I nod. "When I was a kid I didn't have much. My mom she . . .. Let's just say she shouldn't have had kids. But Banks, he and his family kind of took care of me when my own family couldn't. When I was a teenager, it got to a point where his grandmother decided to take me in. She had a way with stubborn teens and looked after Banks, his cousin Darren, and myself. She was hard on us and she insisted that we stay in and do our homework when every other kid in the neighborhood was out on the streets mucking about. I hated it at first, but the lure of good food and safe shelter had me willing to do anything she said to keep that roof over my head. So Banks, Darren, and I would all sit around a tiny kitchen table and we studied from the time we got home from school until Grandma Dee served up dinner. The only sound in that house besides the scratching of pencil against paper where Grandma Dee's knitting needles. Click-clack click-clack. It was kind of like those metronomes music teachers use to help you keep the beat. Click-clack click-clack. If it wasn't for her, I wouldn't be where I am today. She saved me. She supported me. She taught me how to be a better man."

"That's beautiful," Becca whispers. "She must be very proud of you, of both of you."

"She was. She's passed now."

"I'm so sorry."

"Thank you. One of the first things Banks and I did was get her out of that cruddy neighborhood. We pulled everyone out of there we could."

"Sounds like there are some people you wish you didn't have to leave behind."

"Not everyone wants to change. They're addicted to their own suffering." I reach out and brush my fingers lightly along the side of her jaw and she puts her knitting down to lean into me.

"Not everybody can be helped."

Tilting my mouth up to the side, I let my hand drop

as I release a breath. "Enough talk of shitty things," I say. "I actually asked you to stay back for a reason. A personal one."

She twists her body toward me and smiles. "I like the sound of this."

"I'm glad. Because I've planned a date for us."

"A date? When?"

I hold my hand out and pull her closer. "Right Now. I plan to take you out, show you a good time, and win your heart all in the space of a few hours."

"Sounds like a tall order. But from what I've seen since meeting you, Ronan Kennedy, if any man in New York City can pull it off, it'll be you." She places her hand on my arm and takes a deep breath, her eyes lighting up. "But before we go, I have something for you."

"What is it?" I ask.

"Close your eyes and hold out your hands."

"OK." I do as she says, my ears straining to hear any clues as I listen to her moving.

"Open," she says eventually, and the moment the softness hits my fingers, I already know.

"Cashmere," I start, grinning down at the item in my hands. "It's perfect."

BECCA

"What do you think?" Ronan says, gesturing to the finished scarf I just gifted him, now wrapped around his neck.

"Just as good as a bought one," I say, borrowing the turn of phrase from my dad.

"Better, actually. You made it. And you started making it during a time where you didn't even think I liked you, so it means a lot."

"To be honest, I was hoping giving you a gift would at least level us up from grunts and short sentences to full sentences and the occasional pleasantry."

"I was only short with you because I couldn't trust myself not to say something inappropriate for the office," he explains, flashing me a smile as he gestures for me to enter Banked Up.

"You could've been as inappropriate as you liked. I wouldn't have minded."

"If only I'd known," he growls, leaning in and nuzzling me behind the ear as we step into the noisy bar. This is the first time we've come in here since we so dramatically left Pierce Goodman a week ago, so when he steps away from me, I'm instantly filled with nerves.

"Do you think anyone will say anything?"

"What about?"

"Ah, us. The way we left Pierce Goodman."

"They won't get a chance even if they wanted to." He smiles.

"What do you mean?"

"I mean, keep your coat on because we're headed to the roof."

Taking a concealed exit, we make our way up a set of stairs then back out into an icy blast of air caused not by the wind, but by . . . a *helicopter.*

"What on earth?"

"Your chariot awaits, madame," Ronan gestures with his hand toward the helicopter, a ridiculously adorable grin on his face as he does so.

"Where are we going?"

"To dinner."

"In a helicopter?"

"How else would we get to where we need to go while also taking an aerial tour of Manhattan at night?"

"This is too much, Ronan," I practically yell as we get closer to the chopper. "I love it."

Seated side by side in the passenger bay, Ronan and I

communicate via headset while we ohhh and ahhh and listen to the pilot talk about what we can see below. The Statue of Liberty, Ellis Island, the Chrysler Building, and the Empire State Building. We see Times Square, the Intrepid, and Central Park. And although I've seen all of these sights before, from up here at night, it's like a whole new world and experience.

"This is amazing!" I say, laughing from all the fun I'm having.

Ronan lifts my hand to his mouth and kisses my knuckles. "There's no one else I'd want to share this with." Swoon.

When we touch down, it's not back on top of the bar where we lifted off. It's on another building all together, to have dinner at a restaurant that you can only get access to via helicopter. A waiter is ready as soon as we alight and ushers us to a candlelit table for two.

"This is ridiculous," I say, the smile hurting my cheeks as I look around. It's almost like we have this whole place to ourselves. "How did you even know this existed?"

"It's one of those places some of the wealthy execs like to flex over. Normally I'm not a super flashy guy, but this sounded like a hell of a lot of fun. I wanted to share the experience with you."

"You've never been here before?"

"Nope. I've never had anyone special enough to bring."

I press my lips together as I feel my entire body flush

under his gaze. Ronan Kennedy has quickly gone from the Jerk of Wall Street to the man of my dreams, and while I'm not usually so eager to jump into bed with someone on the first date, I've already made my mind up that Ronan is going to be the exception to that. I don't want to wait when already this feels too good to be true.

Instead, I want to grab on with both hands and enjoy whatever this is for as long as I can. Maybe my dad would call me a sellout, but the opportunity to be wooed by a gorgeous multi-millionaire who looks at me like I'm the sun to his moon doesn't tend to present itself too often. So I don't want to question this. I just want to live and bask in the glorious moment. No negativity. Just fun— I'm not even going to question why a man this gorgeous would be this interested in a woman this round. The math doesn't add up, so I've decided I must be living in a fantasy. Like, it's possible that when Ronan confronted me about the offer to change teams, I got so flustered that I passed out, and now I'm still on his office floor dreaming of a perfect future that seems heavily inspired by Jerry McGuire and the Hallmark channel. I've heard those things can happen to people, that they can live a lifetime of memories in the ten seconds they're out. So I figure, if it's that, I'm in for a wild ride and I hope they don't wake me up too soon.

"I like that you feel that way, Ronan," I whisper, lifting my glass of wine and taking a sip as I stare into his eyes. "It means a lot for me to learn the way you've been feeling toward me and to have you confide in me about your past too. It makes me realize that there are some things I need to tell you too. Namely, I feel that I need to explain my relationship with Peter Greer."

"Please. Let me stop you there. Whatever was going on between you and Greer doesn't need to affect you and me now. I admit that at first, I was pissed at the guy but now that his actions have pushed me to do something I should have done a long time ago, I'm grateful to him. With this new direction, we get to have our careers, and each other too." He reaches across the table and laces his fingers with mine. "Dance with me."

Pulling me to my feet, he leads me to the vacant space between the tables and gently sways with me from side to side. The woodsy scent of his cologne and masculine heat fills my senses and has me practically melting against him. I'm normally a big fan of dessert after dinner, but all I really want is to get the hell out of here and invite him to spend the night in my apartment.

Which is exactly what I do.

The helicopter lands on the roof of my building, and like the gentleman he is, Ronan walks me to my door. I haven't done the inviting him in part yet, and I'm so touched that he seems ready to just kiss me and say good night if that's all I want. There's hunger in his eyes, but he's not pushing me.

"Don't go home tonight," I whisper, wrapping my hand around his tie as he brings his mouth to mine.

"Are you sure?"

"Certain," I breathe, releasing a whimper as his mouth lands on mine and he steps in with me through the door, kicking it closed behind us with a thud. And that's pretty much where Ronan's restraint ends . . .

BECCA

With fumbling fingers, I pull his tie loose and shove his coat and jacket to the floor, getting to work on the buttons of his shirt while he does the same to me, our mouths never leaving each other's. It's like I've forgotten the layout to my apartment as we walk backward, kissing, touching, stripping. Instead of directing him to the bedroom, we land against the wall somewhere in my living area and just stay there.

"I've run this moment through my head about a thousand times since I met you, cashmere. And not one of those times measures up to the reality of it." His eyes move over my body as I stand with my back against the wall wearing nothing but a set of deep purple and black lace-trimmed underwear. "You look good enough to eat."

"So do you," I whisper, reaching out and running my hands over his taut pecs and multiplying my luck with the number of abs clearly defined on his lean stomach. I read once that the reason some muscular men enjoy plumper women is because they like our pillowy softness compared to their firmness. And as his hands lift to cup my breasts, thumbs dancing over my puckered nipples, I'm more than happy to be his soft pillowy goodness. His touch is divine.

"I need to taste you, sweet girl," he rasps as he lowers to his knees in front of me then rakes his fingers down over my belly, easing his fingers into the waistband of my panties and dragging them down my legs. "I want to fuck you with my tongue."

Dropping my head back against the wall, I moan as he sweeps his tongue through my soaking seam, my entire body trembling with longing and desire when he focuses on my clit and sucks and swirls. Obviously wanting better access, he hooks a strong arm behind my knee and lifts my leg so it's draping over his shoulder. My fingers go into his hair as his tongue moves lower, spearing into me before flattening out and returning to my clit.

"That feels so good," I gasp, my hips rocking in time as he repeats the movement, making my whole world feel like it's spinning.

"So sweet," he murmurs, his words muffled as he continues to eat me out like a man starved. Two of his fingers take over from his tongue and curl into my insides as he focuses his mouth on my clit and really drives me wild. I can't hold it any longer.

"Ronan!" I call out, my orgasm hitting like a wave

crashing over me, rocking my body and causing my limbs to turn into jelly. Ronan has hold of me, but I somehow manage to slither down the wall, ending up on the floor feeling completely boneless. "Oh fuck."

Ronan kisses his way up my body, chuckling slightly as he holds himself over me. "Feel good?"

I nod, a stupid but sated grin taking over my face from where I lie on the wooden floor, cool against my back. "That release was months' worth of being forced to look and feeling like I'd never touch," I say, running my hands down his strong arms.

"Why would you never be able to touch?" he asks, looking as though he genuinely doesn't understand the thought process. "Because of the company policy?"

"Not only that. I just never imagined a man like you would look twice at a girl like me."

"A girl like you?" he asks, rocking back to his knees and unzipping his pants while I watch every movement with rapt attention. "You mean a *woman* who makes me so hard I'm almost coming on the inside of my pants from looking at you?"

"I can get on board with that train of thought," I say, pressing up on my elbows as I watch him shuck the last of his clothes and take his long, thick cock in hand. There's something so deliciously masculine about watching the lusty haze take over a man's eyes when he pumps his cock while looking at you. It feels empowering, like you're all they can see and the only thing in this world they want.

"You like seeing what you do to me?"

"Uh-huh."

"I've jacked off like this a thousand times thinking about you," he admits, his hand moving back and forth, slow and firm. He hisses through his teeth. "I used to imagine bending you over my desk and lifting those heavy woolen skirts over your head and just fucking you until you scream."

"Is that why you seemed put out when I started wearing the fitted suits?" I smile, panting while I watch him, my insides aching for him to enter me.

He laughs slightly. "They only made me want you more."

"Then what are you waiting for?" I widen my legs for him, loving the rumbling grunt that leaves his chest as his eyes drop to my soaking core. "Take what you want. Unless you want me bent over a desk?"

"No. I want you right here on the fucking floor," he says, shifting forward and positioning his tip at my entrance, teasing me for a moment before he plunges right in.

"Holy fuck!" I call out, my head lulling back as heat, desire, and a touch of pain flood me as he fills me with his size. "You're so fucking big."

"And you're so fucking perfect," he rasps, moving his hips and driving back and forth inside me.

RONAN

I don't think I've ever wanted a woman as much as I want Becca. From the moment I found her crouched over her broken cactus and unraveled knitting, until this moment now where I'm finally inside her, I've been infatuated. While working at Pierce Goodman, I knew I'd never be able to act on my impulses, and as much as I tried to move past them—to get over her—I just couldn't. Somehow, her sweet and innocent smile, her sharp and witty mind, and her ability to make every one of my days better burrowed so deep under my skin that she was and is the only person I can see. The moment I was at risk of losing her in any capacity was the moment I knew I had to act or risk losing her forever. And now that she's mine, gasping under me while her insides clamp tight around my cock, I know that I'll do whatever it takes to keep her always.

This girl—this woman—is mine and mine only.

"You feel so fucking amazing, baby," I grunt, my body moving inside her with abandon. My skin burns and muscles feel tight, my burgeoning release growing heavy in my balls, hot in my spine as her hips buck up and meet me thrust for thrust.

"Oh God! Ronan. I can't. This is too much. It's so good. I can't hold it. *Ronan!*" Her nails claw at my skin and her desperate words flood all of my senses, causing the flood gates to open and for me to bury myself with one last deep thrust, spilling myself inside her as the ferocity of my release causes blood to go rushing through my ears like thunder in a storm.

"Now *that* was months' worth of being forced to look and not touch," I tease, smiling as I lean over her and press my mouth to hers, kissing her languidly as I move inside her gently, bringing us both down from that dizzying high.

"I love that you've wanted me for as long as I wanted you," she whispers, her arms circling my neck as our mouths taste tenderly, bodies heaving and relaxing.

I pause and press my forehead to hers, wanting desperately to say something back, a certain four-letter word swimming through my head and my heart but stalling somewhere on its way out of my mouth. I want to tell her I'm in love with her. That I think I've been in love with her since that first day, but instead, I press my mouth to hers again, kissing her in a way that I hope conveys what I wish I could say out loud but can't. Not yet, anyway . . .

BECCA

"So, what do you think the policy for inter office relations is going to be at Kennedy and Co?" I ask Ronan as I make a show of sitting on the edge of his desk, so my chest is eye level to where he sits. The smirk and the lingering gaze at the lacy edges of my camisole peeking from my blouse tells me the move doesn't go unnoticed.

"I think that as long as there's no abuse of power and relationships don't get in the way of work then anything goes."

"Good. Because I've been thinking about that fantasy you mentioned."

"The one where I bend you over my desk?"

"Yeah." I giggle. I can't help myself. Accepting the reality of being in a full-blown relationship with the hottest guy I've ever known is a bit of a head spin for me. And after a weekend filled with delectable bedroom activities, I'm the epitome of cloud nine. "I kind of wanna try that."

"Is that a fact?" Ronan's brow quirks, his eyes taking a slow perusal of my body before they suddenly shift toward the doorway. "Good morning, Scott." He smiles and I jump up quickly, feeling a bit like a kid caught with their hand in the cookie jar as I make sure my blouse and skirt are sitting straight.

Scott freezes and looks between us, a slow smirk taking over his mouth as he nods. "You two are fucking."

"Fucking is a bit crass for my taste. But yes, Rebecca and I are together. Do you have any problems with this?"

"Nope." Scott's eyes move from Ronan to me, his smile getting wider as my blush grows hotter. "None at all. In fact, I celebrate this union—as long as I don't have to listen to any shenanigans during the workday."

"We'll be consummate professionals," Ronan assures him.

"OK. Well, I need to borrow Becca so we can get ready for our first pitch meeting. Is that OK?"

"She's all yours," Ronan says, gesturing magnanimously as I make my way toward the door. "Oh, Rebecca?"

"Yes?" I say, stilling in the doorway.

"The idea you had. I'd like to take you up on it. See me before the end of the day and we'll get it into the schedule."

I don't know why, but combining office and sex talk is ridiculously appealing, and I have to press my knees together as a flood of hormones threatens to buckle them. "Will do, boss."

Scott gives it about thirty seconds of us setting up for the pitch before he starts with the questions.

"When did this happen? You know I'm dying of jealousy."

I bite the inside of my lip so I don't smile too hard or burst into a fit of girly giggles or something.

"It started the first day here. After you left, we got to talking and . . . one thing led to another—"

"And now you're bangin' the boss. You know, I didn't think you had it in you, but my god, I'm so proud. I'll bet he fucks as hard as he works too. He has that, 'I can get you off with my pinky finger' vibe going on."

The heat in my cheeks is an inferno by now. "Let's just say I have zero complaints."

"Ah, I knew it. My boyfriend met him at the work Christmas party and said that if I ever had a free pass it'd be for Ronan. He just oozes sex appeal, so he could understand a loss of restraint with that level of manliness aimed at you. But I also think he'll be relieved the man is now taken—not that I had a chance, but a boy can dream, right?"

"I guess so." I laugh. "I'm sorry to burst your bubble."

"Noooo. Don't be sorry. I'm teasing! I'm super fucking happy for you. He seems smitten over you, which totally explains a lot of his behavior over these past few months."

"What do you mean?"

"Well, I don't think I need to point out the knitting again. But other than that, he just seemed calmer. Possibly a little distracted, but calmer. Probably why your brother thought it was OK to try and steal you. Have you spoken to him yet?"

I shake my head. "I've been dodging his calls. I really need to explain everything about that to Ronan. But whenever it comes up, he always changes the subject."

"Yikes. Well, you'd better get on top of that or it's likely to blow up in your face. It's a good thing Ronan won, though. And once we win these pitches and start raking in our returns, we'll be winning too. Imagine how red in the face Katerina and Angel will be when they see us more successful than them. I can't wait to run into them twelve months from now and rub our success in their faces."

"Sounds like you're holding a grudge," I say, grinning.

"They're awful people, so it's a reasonable grudge for sure."

After I finish checking the big monitor's connectivity, I place the remote in the center of the table then head to the kitchen to fill a jug with iced water.

"You won't be needing that," Ronan says from behind me, his deep voice startling and turning me on at the same time.

"Why? What happened?" I ask, shutting off the water and setting the jug aside.

"Pitch called and cancelled. Said they decided to go another way."

"Another way? What way? Don't they know who you are? There's no better way than with you," I blunder, confusion muddling my brain. Back at Pierce Goodman, I was fighting people off left, right, and center because they all wanted Ronan Kennedy on their investment team. He could take a project and turn a profit faster than any other VC in the company or in the entire financial district. Cancelling and going another way doesn't make any sense.

"It's OK. Sometimes people get cold feet. We'll get the next one," he says, taking the news way better than I expected.

"You're not disappointed?"

He moves to stand in front me, his hands resting on my hips as he pulls me closer to him. "I would be. But I've got something better to look forward to today when we're alone. Nothing's going to kill my buzz."

"Why do you think I wore the pleated skirt?" I say, twisting slightly from side to side.

He looks down and growls. "And why do you think my dick's been impossibly hard since you walked into my office before?"

It's my turn to look down. The end of the work day can't come fast enough.

RONAN

With my fingers digging into the fleshiness at her hips, I slowly drag my cock in and out of her, savoring this moment so the reality of it can be etched into my mind always. No matter how many times I fantasized about bending Becca over my desk, those fantasies never quite measured up to the sublime experience it really is. I'm never going to be able to look at this desk without becoming aroused again.

"Oh fuck. Ronan. Yes. That's so good," she moans, her hands gripping the opposite edge as I bury myself deep. *Thrust, draw back, thrust.* "I want more."

"More, you say?"

"Uh-huh," she gasps, turning her head slightly so she can meet my eyes. "Fuck me like you mean it."

Something about her words create a surge of need inside me, spurring me on and quickening my pace and force. The desk rocks, the cup holding my pens toppling and falling to the floor as I rock her world along with the furniture.

"Ronan! Yes! Yeeesssss!"

We come together with a shudder and a moan, and I'm quick to lean over her and kiss her face, her hair, as my body tremors with the final pulses of my release. "You're a dream come true, Rebecca."

"I could say the same for you," she gasps, turning to face me as I ease myself out of her and we get cleaned up. "Why do you call me that, by the way?"

My eyes lift to meet hers as I finish tightening my belt buckle. "Call you what? Cashmere?"

"No, Rebecca. Everyone else calls me Becca or Bec. But you've always used my full name."

"At first," I start, sliding my hand around her waist and pulling her against my body as I reach up with the other hand and tuck her unruly curls behind her ear, "it was me trying to overcome my reaction to you and view you in a professional light. I toyed with referring to you as Miss Maxwell for a while too, but neither worked. And then that's just who you became to me. I like calling you something no one else does. Does it bother you?"

"No," she whispers. "I just wanted to know the reason."

"Slowly learning all of my idiosyncrasies, huh?"

"Oh, I think I know most of them. It's how I managed to be the only assistant you didn't fire in the first month."

"And you know I tried to find a reason to. I didn't like

how out of control I felt around you." I stare into her eyes, fondly reliving those early tense moments where I felt almost panicked whenever I thought I might be alone with her. I just didn't trust myself at all.

"Is it bad that I love that I make you lose control?"

"No. I'm learning to love losing control with you too." Leaning in closer, I brush my lips to hers then kiss her slow and soft, my tongue tenderly sweeping along hers before finishing with a gentle pull of her bottom lip between my teeth. "You drive me wild."

"Why do I feel like there's a 'but' coming along?"

"No 'but'. Just a disappointed acceptance of the fact I have to work late tonight."

"I can wait up for you if you want to crash at my place later. It's closer to here than yours, so you'll get more sleep for all your meetings tomorrow."

"More sleep? Sweet girl, if I'm in bed with you, the last thing I can think about is sleep."

"Oh. Is that a no to coming over then?"

"It's a no to sleep. I'll definitely be coming home to you."

"I like the sound of that. You sure you don't want me to hang around? I can set up and knit in the corner."

"As much as I love that idea, I think I just need to focus tonight. I'll call you when I'm on my way though."

"OK," she says, a tiny smile curving her lips as she leans in and plants a kiss to my lips. "I'll see you later then."

"You can count on it."

Taking a slow step back from me, she gives me an adorable finger wave before turning and walking out of the office. I hear the front door open and close and then I get to work straightening up my desk and picking up the pens and the handful of papers that also fell to the floor.

By the time I'm ready to go, I settle myself back in my chair and power up my computer again, clicking straight onto the email client out of habit. And that's when I see them. My entire week's worth of meetings, cancelled. Shit.

"That motherfucker," I mutter, slamming my laptop closed and dropping my head against the back of my chair. There's only one person who'd go out of their way to make things harder for me, and this time Banks isn't around to talk me out of going and punching him in the face.

BECCA

Walking up to my apartment, I pause when I find Peter standing out in the cool night air waiting for me, his coat collar pulled high about his neck.

"If you bothered wearing any of the scarves I've knitted you over the years, you wouldn't feel so cold right now."

"I'd be a hell of a lot warmer inside, but it seems your concierge has orders not to let me in," he says, thumbing over his shoulder as he moves toward where I'm standing. "Ronan's doing, I suppose?"

"Well, he does own the apartment. And he doesn't like you. So I'm really not surprised."

Peter smirks at that. "You're a kept woman now?"

I take a small step back. "I pay my rent."

"Market value?" His brow lifts in question and I roll my eyes, sighing as I look away from him.

"I'm still mad at you, Pete. So why don't you just get to the point of why you're here?"

"I think you're making a horrible mistake leaving the company to work with Ronan," he tells me. "But if you'll come back and work for me, I can still salvage your career. It's not too late."

I roll my eyes. "After everything you've gone and done behind my back?"

"What exactly have I done?" he asks, sounding genuinely curious.

"Used me as a pawn in your little game to one-up Ronan. I'm your sister, Pete. You could have told me what was going on instead of planting me on Ronan's team then just expecting I'd tell you everything going on. That's not cool."

"I wasn't asking you to do anything illegal," Peter says defensively. "I just wanted to understand how he operates. Ronan is the best and I'd be a fool to pass up the opportunity to learn from him."

"Then why didn't you just ask him instead of using me?"

"Because he would have laughed at me," Peter retorts. "You know how Ronan operates, Becca. He's got an ego bigger than Central Park, and the arrogance to match. The man isn't very forthcoming when asked how and why he makes his decisions. So if you think he'd ever show me anything I could use to beat him in any way . . . well, then you're a fool."

I shake my head at that. "No, Pete. You're the fool if

you honestly believe that him being better than you meant you needed to be mortal enemies who try and screw each other over at every turn. I know it was you who got that pitch canceled today. Don't even pretend it wasn't."

"You got me," he says, sighing. "Yes, I was the one who stopped the pitch. I offered them a far better deal than Ronan could with his limited resources."

"Why would you do that? Why can't you just let this go? He's left the company now. Without him there, you'll get promoted to senior partner with no competition."

"Because I didn't win, Bec. It doesn't count if you aren't the actual best, and to do that, I need to prove that without the massive backing of Pierce Goodman, Ronan's skills aren't worth shit."

"If you ruin his business before it even gets off the ground by using underhanded tactics, then you still aren't the best. You're just a cheat."

He presses his lips together in a tight line, obviously lacking a response.

"This is why I'd never play Monopoly with you. You were always so damn competitive. But I need to you back off here. Please."

"Why would I do that?"

My heart tightens in my chest as I force the words I've only allowed myself to think out of my mouth. "Because I'm in love with him."

Pete balks. "What? No. Not him, Bec. Anyone but him."

"Why can't it be him?"

"Because he's the biggest jerk on Wall St."

"Not to me he isn't."

"Jesus. You're serious here, aren't you? You actually love the guy?"

"I do."

He runs his hand through his hair and shakes his head. "Fine."

"Fine?"

"Yeah, fine. I'll back off. But if he hurts you . . ." He doesn't finish the threat and just lets it hang in the air. But I know what it means. It's the big brother way of saying, hurt my little sister and I'll make you regret it.

"Thank you, Pete," I whisper, taking a step closer then rising up on my toes to press a chaste kiss to his cheek. "You can be an OK guy when you wanna be."

"Yeah, don't tell anyone," he says with a crooked smile before he turns away. "I wish you the best of luck with him, Bec. You'll need it."

"Thanks," I say with a short-lived smile, because before I even know what's happening, a fist comes flying out of nowhere and clocks Peter on the side of the jaw. *Oof!*

"Get the fuck away from her!" Ronan growls, standing over Pete who literally went down like a sack of bricks.

"Ronan! No!" I shout, reaching for him. He flinches out of the way, his eyes finding mine and looking tortured.

"What is he doing here?"

"This isn't what you think," I gasp desperately.

"I was just here to talk to my *sister*," Pete groans, clutching his jaw as he gets up clumsily.

"What?" Ronan stumbles back. "You're . . . you're siblings? What the? Why did you keep this from me?" His eyes turn to me, accusing.

"I tried to tell you, Ronan. I wanted to tell you. But at first I couldn't, and then I just didn't get the chance. When I tried you cut me off and said you didn't want to know."

"So, this has been you two all along? Are you . . . were you conspiring against me this whole time?"

"What?" My eyes go wide and I look from Ronan to Pete and back again. "No! I'd never. I had no idea . . . Pete. Tell him!"

"I put her in your team as plant," he admits. "But she—"

Pete doesn't get to finish before Ronan's fist lashes out again and puts Pete on his ass. "I'll stay at my own place tonight," he grunts, chest heaving as he glances at me with dark and stormy eyes, his hands clenched by his side as he stalks away.

"Ronan! It wasn't like that! I didn't know!" I call after him, torn between rushing after him and tending to the now passed out Pete. "Shit." Duty wins over and I crouch down beside my brother and tap his face until he opens his eyes again.

"Wha— What? What happened?" he mumbles incoherently.

"You're an idiot. That's what happened," I say, helping him to his feet then up to my apartment so I can make sure he doesn't have a concussion while I have an anxiety attack over the state of my relationship.

RONAN

Raking my hand back and forth through my hair, I pace the living room of my brownstone, my phone pressed to my ear as I try and get a hold of Banks. I need his advice. I need his guidance, but most of all, I just really need a friendly ear. I feel so betrayed. Peter is Rebecca's brother? And he put her on my team as a plant? I don't know if I'm dumb, or if I just fell for the greatest con job in history. This could ruin me.

I fell in love with her.

I think that's the worst part too. In my life, there have been very few people I felt connected to. Having grown up with an absentee mother and never knowing my father, I sought solace in others, and others didn't always have the best of intentions. Except for Banks and his family. They became the family I never thought I could have, and it wasn't until I met Rebecca that I even considered creating something of my own. But now it turns out she was working against me and I don't know what to do.

Giving up when Banks's phone goes through to voicemail, I toss it on the couch and rake my hands through my hair yet again. My eyes immediately land on the bottle of vodka in the bar, and I head straight for it, figuring the bottom of that is as good a place to find myself as any. It's not like I have a business to go to in the morning.

Pouring myself a stiff drink, I sit on the edge of the couch and try to make sense of everything. I feel like I've been punched in the gut. It hurts more than when my mom walked out on me. At least then I knew it was coming. This? This was a sucker punch I never even saw coming.

I never even knew Peter had a sister.

And yet, she was there for me just when I was giving up hope, and it was like she was an angel sent to me from heaven to help me with work and life in general. I'd been feeling so full of directionless anger before she came to work for me, but within a few weeks of her around, I actually started looking forward to getting up and going to work each day just so I could see her.

But it was all a sham.

She was only there to spy on me and report back to her brother.

The more I drink, the angrier I get. I want to go after Peter the way he came after me, tear him down and ruin his career without even batting an eyelid. And what's worse, I want to do the same to her. I want her to feel the same amount of pain I do right now, because falling for someone—*trusting* someone—only to find out they've been working against you is freaking heartbreaking.

Downing the last of my drink, I get up for another refill when I hear a knock at the door. I half expect it to be Banks coming to see why I called him so many times, but when I pull the door open and find Rebecca on the stoop, all of my anger and resolve fades away and all that's left is gut-wrenching hurt.

"I don't have anything to say to you," I force out, moving to close the door on her before she can speak.

"But I have something to say to you," she argues, placing her hand against the door and trying to push it open.

Looking down at her hand, all I can think is that her touch was so loving and caring just a few hours ago, but now that memory feels like poison. Her sweet words are lies, everything about what we've built together is a lie, and that's just too much to handle.

"I don't want to hear it."

"I don't care. You're going to listen because you have this all wrong. I was *never* spying on you."

With my jaw locked, I straighten my spine as I step to the side, letting her into the foyer if only to save us both from advertising my naivety to the neighbors.

"You have five minutes," I say bluntly, looking at my watch before I move back over to the bar and pour myself another drink.

"I only need a couple," she says, following me. "Peter acted alone, and the moment I found out what he was doing, I told him no. I wanted no part of it."

"But you didn't think to warn me?"

"We left the company shortly after. I didn't see the sense. We were so focused on generating a client base that I didn't even stop to consider that Pete would come after you again—especially with me working with you. I thought it would all end when we were out of the building."

"I don't think you understand just how deep my rivalry with your brother goes."

"I think I have a pretty good idea after tonight," she says quietly, her eyes locking with mine.

My heart jolts because there's so much pain there, and for a minute I'm tempted to believe her, to let myself just forget everything I've learned and trust her again. But the anger and hurt is still too raw, too fresh, and I can't quite bring myself to close the distance between us and draw her into my arms.

"Is he at least OK?" I ask, my knuckles still hurting from the two hits I gave him earlier.

"He's fine. I gave him some ice and sent him home not long ago. He's not pressing any charges . . . just so you know."

"I honestly don't give a shit if he does. He's already taken everything from me."

"About that, Ronan. I asked him to back off and leave you be. If he wants to best you at this game, then he'll have to do it above board. No more stealing or threatening clients."

I lift my glass to my mouth, but I don't take a sip. "And he agreed?"

She bounces a shoulder and steps closer to me, a tiny smile tugging at her mouth. "I threatened to tattle on him to our dad. And let me tell you, no one wants Reg Greer to feel disappointed in them. That man can lecture like it's nobody's business."

A smile quirks the side of my mouth as I take a sip of bitter liquid. "I think I like your dad already."

"Yeah? I think he'd like you too. He'd appreciate the way you followed your heart and started your own business. You know, everyone says I take after him. Pete takes after my mom."

My eyes narrow slightly. "Why am I getting the feeling that that's a bad thing?"

"Because my mom left us to go chase some rich guy and move to the Bahamas. We haven't seen her in years."

"That's a shame."

"Not as far as I'm concerned."

"No. It's a shame for her. She's missing out on you. A trap I have to admit I just almost allowed myself to fall into."

For a minute, we just stare at each other and I can feel the anger dissipating. The hurt is still there, but it's manageable now that I know she wasn't working against me like I thought.

"Why did you hide it for so long?" I finally ask, my voice softer than before.

"The fact that Pete and I are related?" I nod as she fidgets with her fingers in front of me. "The company policy was to never have family members work together, but he pulled some strings so I was allowed to work there, and part of that was agreeing to keep it all on the down low. I guess I just got so used to not mentioning it that I didn't think it pertinent until he made it an issue with his actions."

"And why did you hide it from me?"

"It's not like that," she protests quickly. "I wasn't hiding anything. I did try to tell you a couple of times, but when you cut me off, I figured maybe it was a sign. I just didn't want our relationship to be influenced by something my idiot brother did. We were new, and we were so good together. I didn't want anything to mess that up."

Reaching out, I brush my thumb over the back of her hand. "We're *still* good together," I murmur. "I just hate that I didn't know sooner. It's a pretty big thing to not tell me."

She nods, chewing on her bottom lip as she stares at our joined hands. "I'll make it up to you, I promise. I'll deal with my knucklehead brother."

It's the last part that almost makes me laugh, but I manage to hold it back, squeezing her hand instead. "I know, you will. And I'm sorry for hitting before asking questions."

"Ahh, he kinda deserved it," Becca says before she exhales loudly then smiles up at me again. "I guess I should probably head out and let you get some rest or whatever. Big day trying to reverse what Pete did tomorrow." She turns to leave then pauses and rises to the tip of her toes and presses a soft kiss against my cheek. "Good night, Ronan."

My hand tightens around hers. "Don't go. Please."

"Oh thank God," she breathes, her hand landing on her chest. "I already sent my driver home and I have an overnight bag outside on the stoop. I was so sure we'd kiss and make up and everything would be OK, but you had me worried there."

"Had me worried too," I say with a chuckle, tugging her in close so I can slide my hand along the underside of her jaw. "But we forgot one very important part."

"What's that?"

"The kissing," I say, bringing my mouth to hers and letting the last shreds of stress melt away as I lose myself in the woman I'm most definitely falling in love with.

BECCA

With a box of raspberry and white chocolate muffins and a blanket I finished knitting my dad yesterday, I make my way off the Staten Island ferry and search Dad's face out in the crowd.

"Sweetheart! It's so good to see you," he says, pulling me into his arms and hugging me tight. "That new job of yours has been keeping you so busy I feel like I haven't seen you in a year."

"Well, it's been months, so close enough," I say, handing him the homemade treats. "Hence why I come bearing gifts. This one is muffins—I took up baking too—and the other is a blanket for you. I know how you prefer to turn the heat down and rug up instead, and the weather just isn't getting warm enough yet."

"No sense in throwing good money away so I can wander around buck naked," he crows, sliding an arm around my shoulders and walking out until we reach his car.

On the journey to his place, he asks me about my work and probes a little into the rift that's developed between me and Peter. It's been a couple of weeks since that blow-up outside my apartment, and while I'm not holding a grudge against him, I'm definitely still annoyed. He jeopardized my relationship with Ronan for his own gain. Sure, we worked it out and we're going stronger than ever, but I still don't think Pete understands the gravity of how much that hurt me.

"Well, I hope you can put aside your differences for one night," Dad says and he pulls into his driveway. "Because your brother is joining us for dinner tonight too. And I'd like it if we could just eat and enjoy each other's company as a family without all that work nonsense getting in the way."

"It wasn't just work nonsense, Dad. Ronan and I almost broke up over it."

"Ah, but you didn't."

"No. Seems he likes me more than he dislikes Pete."

"Smart man that Ronan. When do you think I'll meet him?"

My cheeks heat as I think about what a monumental step that would be. "When I know how serious we are."

"Serious enough to walk out of an upscale job."

"Well, I was raised by a man who taught me that integrity was more important than money, and I felt that supporting Ronan as he builds his own company was the right thing to do."

"Doesn't hurt that the guy's dreamy though, right?" Dad says, waggling his eyebrows comically and making me laugh.

"Oh my god, you are ridiculous," I say as I get out of the car and head inside. Pete's already in the living room when I arrive.

"Hey, sis," he says, getting up from the couch to greet me. I can see the genuine warmth in his eyes. "Good to see you."

"You too, I suppose," I say, feeling a little stiff as I embrace him. "How have you been?"

"Atoning for my sins. I'm unlikely to make senior partner anymore, but I'm learning to be OK with that."

"Oh?" My brow shoots up and I want to ask more questions, but Dad clears his throat to remind us that business talk is off-limits. "Should we eat?"

"Definitely," Pete says, gesturing for me to walk ahead of him to the kitchen."

"I don't know about you but I'm freaking famished."

The rest of the evening is spent eating, talking, and catching up on each other's lives. Dad's enthusiastic when I tell him more about Ronan's company and the part I play in making that happen. Pete stays quiet through it all, which might be because he feels bad for putting me in a position where I could have lost my job and my relationship. Or maybe he really is learning something from his mistakes. Either way, my dad seems overjoyed at having both of his children together under the same roof.

"It's been so long since we've done this," Dad says as he helps me clear the table. "I'm glad you came to visit. I really am."

"Me too, Dad," I say, glancing into the living area where Pete is still sitting. "And I'm glad you invited Pete along too. I think we needed this."

"Despite all our differences, we're still family. And we've got to stick together. There isn't a lot of us left."

"You're right. And I promise to make an effort to visit more often from now on."

"I'd like that. Just be sure to bring that man of yours too. I'd like to judge him for myself."

"I'm sure. But I can promise he's more than worthy. Actually, he's really wonderful. He's the reason I got out of that awful apartment so early. I didn't even know until right before we started dating."

"Well, I'm grateful to him for that. I hated thinking of you in that place. That building should be condemned."

"My friend Nina would agree wholeheartedly with you on that one."

"Who's Nina?" Pete butts in, grabbing an apple from the fruit bowl and taking a massive bite.

"A friend of mine from Pierce Goodman."

"Haven't you eaten enough tonight?" Dad laughs.

"I'm a growing boy."

"You're a thirty-nine-year-old man."

Pete laughs then turns his blue eyes to me. "I'm about to head out. Wanna hitch a ride?"

"You OK with all this?" I ask, gesturing to the mess from dinner and offering Dad the dish towel.

He takes it from me. "Of course. You both get home safe and I'll see you soon. Understood?"

"Yes, sir," I say, giving him a hug before following Pete out.

"I really am sorry about how everything went down," Pete says once we're on the road. With my belly full, I sink comfortably into his plush leather seats.

"Are you sorry because you hurt me? Or are you sorry there were consequences and you ended up hurting yourself?"

He turns to me and flashes a grin. "Can I be both?"

I roll my eyes but can't help but smile. "Of course you can, you incorrigible ass."

"I'm glad you still think I'm funny."

"I've never stopped thinking that. You're just a giant pain in my ass sometimes."

He laughs and reaches for my hand, giving it a squeeze. "I know. And I'm sorry. I'll try to do better."

"That would be nice," I say, leaning back in the seat and closing my eyes as we head toward the city. It's been a long day, but it's ended on a good note. And that's something to build on.

"I'm glad he makes you happy, sis. Ronan, I mean."

"Thanks, Pete. He really does."

RONAN

"Good morning, beautiful," I murmur, smiling as Becca opens her eyes and slowly focuses on mine.

"Hmm. Good morning, handsome." A sleepy grin curves her mouth as she stretches and rolls against me. "Your bed is ridiculously comfy."

"You slept right through the alarm."

She fully opens her eyes and looks at me properly, registering the fact that I'm already dressed and ready for work. "Ohmygod. Why didn't you wake me? We're gonna be late."

"You were so peaceful," I say with a chuckle. "I didn't have the heart."

"I'm going to make us miss the pitch meeting. And after all the effort and stress we've been through to turn things around, we can't afford to let something as stupid as me sleeping in make us look unprofessional."

"We won't look unprofessional," I say, grinning as she throws the covers back and rushes about the room collecting items of clothing that were strewn about in our haste to get to bed last night.

She turns to me and throws her arms up. "Of course we will. Did you know that this is the main reason I had come to work for Pierce Goodman in the first place? I kept sleeping through my alarm and I got fired from three separate jobs for my lateness." She holds up three fingers but all I'm really doing is focusing on her chest. She has an amazing set of tits and she's buck naked in front of me right now. If this meeting wasn't as important as it is, I'd call and cancel it myself just so I could ravish her in the shower. "Do you seriously have a hard on right now?"

"Yeah." I nod. "You're fucking gorgeous and you're naked, so . . ."

"Men," she gasps, shaking her head and storming into the bathroom. I hear the shower turn on and I head into the kitchen to make her a Keep Cup of coffee and a bagel for the drive to our meeting. I'd much prefer to follow her into the bathroom, but then I'd make good on the desires of my 'other head' and this really would become the economic disaster Becca is making this out as.

While we have called somewhat of a truce with her brother over the last few weeks, it has taken a herculean effort to get us back on track. A couple of clients could be coaxed back, but the others didn't want the drama in their business relationships. I didn't blame them. So it took hours of research and chasing up new leads to find some bigger and better investment opportunities to make our first year of business a profitable one. And if we get today's client—a medicinal cannabis company looking to expand into the global market—to agree to our terms, then it'll elevate Kennedy and Co. to the next level.

I'm still not sure how Becca was able to convince the company's CEO that we were the right team for this project, because every VC in the city is vying for his account. But convincing him of our terms will be a different story. He's a hard-nosed businessman who is used to getting his own way, so Scott, Becca, and I have worked closely to put together an offer he can't refuse, and one that will hopefully pay off for us long term.

Becca was adamant that she wanted to be more than just an assistant on this project, and I have to say, her input has been a breath of fresh air. She has a natural affinity for the work, and now that the tension her brother's misdealings caused has dissipated, we've been able to focus on the task at hand. I can't help but wonder if this is what things will always be like between us—two people with a deep emotional connection and a common goal in sight. One can only hope, because the more time I spend with her, the more I realize she's The One.

I'm brought out of my thoughts by the sound of the shower turning off. I quickly finish making her coffee and meet her as she exits the bedroom with her breakfast in hand. "For the commute. You look beautiful by the way." I drop a kiss on the side of her forehead.

"Thanks," she says, running a hand down her beige skirt before taking the coffee and bagel without breaking a stride on our way out the door. "You know, we might actually make this meeting after all." She flashes a smile as she hops into the car. I grab my laptop and slide in beside her so we can go over strategy on the way.

"So, how do you think we should approach this whole thing?" she asks, munching on her bagel as I set up my laptop on the tablet mount in front of us and turn to face her.

"Well, he's looking for supplementary income right now." She nods as I click through my notes. "He wants to take advantage of his current infrastructure to connect with new markets, so he needs someone who can make that happen."

"OK," Becca says, nodding again. "Our offer will cover all of that, but he might need some convincing over the amount of involvement we want. What is it you're thinking he'll settle for?"

"A mix of equity and stock to get us through the first year of growth. That way we won't have to worry about burning through our funding before everything is in place." A look of concern crosses her face, but it's brief and she quickly recovers.

"Got it." Becca nods, looking thoughtful as she sips her coffee. "What do you think is going to be the biggest roadblock?"

"I'm pretty sure his biggest priority will be being able to oversee everything from a distance. He wants to assure success goes into the right hands before he makes a move." Up ahead I see Scott arriving.

"Scott's here," I say as our driver comes to a stop beside him. "You ready?"

Slotting her coffee into the cup holder, she takes a deep and steadying breath. "Yeah. I'm ready."

The door opens and we both step out, meeting Scott halfway to the door. "I am sweating bullets, right now," he says, his voice sounding a little shaky as we walk into the building. Medican's offices are located on the top floor above their research and distribution facility.

"Ah, perfect timing!" Jacob Nass, Medican's CEO, says as he rounds the corner just as we step off the elevator. "We've only spoken over the phone, but I can already take a guess which one of you is Rebecca. It's lovely to meet you."

"And you, sir," Becca says, a slight blush of excitement on her cheeks. "This is my boss, Ronan Kennedy, and my colleague, Scott Treville. We're so grateful to you for seeing us when we know you have a lot of interest in this."

"Well, I liked the passion and spirit in your voice when we spoke. I remember being young and enthusiastic once, and it's that kind of energy we need to get Medican to the next level."

He gestures for us to follow, and we make our way

into the conference room. Every seat is filled with his senior management team. We all take our seats around the table and an assistant sets paperwork covering their vision in front of each of us to accompany the presentation.

"Thanks again for being willing to come here today," Jacob says, looking between Scott, Becca, and me. "As you're aware, we're looking for a little help in getting our growth strategy off the ground."

"We are," Scott says, his voice steady and his face betraying nothing. I'm having a proud mentor moment here. "And we're excited to offer our services."

Jacob looks down at the papers in front of him before nodding and picking up the first one. "These are the financials for the past year," he starts, flipping through them quickly. "As you can see, our profits have been on a slight decline. We've been trying to expand into new markets, but it's been difficult with our current infrastructure on top of the costs navigating different legislation. We're losing more than we're gaining."

He puts the papers down and leans back in his chair, steepling his fingers together as he looks at us. "What we need is someone who can come in and help us take advantage of current resources to connect with new markets. We're looking for a partner, someone who is willing to take a partial stake in the company and help us grow."

"And that's where we come in," I say. "As you may

have learned from your own research, I have more than enough contacts in logistics and exports to make this happen."

"I also heard you were one half of the team who took over at Wright Media. Their profits are outstanding this quarter. I'm hoping you'll do the same for us."

"It's always a team effort that makes these things work, sir. In the case of Wright Media, a restructure of management made all the difference."

He looks at me for a long moment before nodding. "I'm assuming you have an offer prepared?" he asks.

Scott nods and slides a piece of paper across the table for Jacob to pick up, reading through it quickly. After a few moments he looks up, his face pinched in a frown. "This is different to what we were anticipating."

"We're aware of that," I say calmly. "But we're willing to take a smaller percentage in exchange for full autonomy of the company, you included."

Jacob picks up the paper again and seems to re-read it before looking back at us. "And what about our existing management?" he asks, his voice tense. "I assume they won't be staying on with this transition?"

"That would be up to them," I say carefully, watching his body language. He's clearly concerned about the offer, but I have a good feeling he's willing to take a risk due to my track record.

"So you're willing to go so far as taking over an entire company for a fraction of the profits?" Jacob asks.

"We believe in this company," Scott says firmly. "And we're willing to do whatever it takes to help it grow."

Jacob nods slowly, his face still pinched in a frown. But after a few moments he finally sighs and reaches for the paper, sliding it back across the table to us. "All right," he says, his voice resigned. "You have a deal."

BECCA

I land against the wall in my apartment with a thud, feeling tipsy after an evening spent celebrating with Ronan, Scott, and his boyfriend. I've never really been much of a nightlife person, but with the buzz in my veins from winning Medican as a client, I felt like partying all night.

Now, though, all I want to do is Ronan, and based on the lustful look in his eyes right now—and the fact we're already down to our underwear—all he's interested in is doing me too.

"If no one was watching tonight, I would have taken you on the dance floor," he rasps, his mouth on my neck, his hand moving up my thigh.

"I don't know," I say, laughing drunkenly. "I thought I'd have to fight off Scott and his boyfriend for a moment there. They seemed to find you very interesting."

Ronan pulls away from me slightly and cocks his

brow. "Zero contest. Not sure if you noticed but this"—he grinds his hips against mine to show me how hard he is—"only rises for you," he says, before leaning in to kiss me again.

A moan escapes me as I reach down to cup his hard length through his boxer briefs, loving the way he groans with each measured stroke.

"Why don't you get your ass to the bedroom before I fuck you on the floor again," he says, dragging his finger down the center of my chest in a slow caress.

"You can fuck me anywhere you want. I don't mind," I whisper, adjusting my grip so I can slide my hand inside his shorts, loving the tiny bit of precum that hits my palm as I move my hand down Ronan's shaft.

"God that feels good." He closes his eyes and reaches his hands above me, bracing himself against the wall.

"Still want to move this to the bedroom?" I ask, gliding my hand up and down, quickening my pace.

He groans. "Fuck yeah, I do. I'm about to unman myself and the only place I want to be coming is inside you."

His words instantly turn me on, but as soon as I remove my hand, a tiny voice inside my head asks, 'why?'

"Why me?" I blurt as he takes me by the hand and starts leading me to my room.

"What do you mean?" He seems genuinely confused.

"I saw women—and men—tonight while we were out. You could have anyone in this city, and yet the person you choose to come home with is me. The dowdy assistant who likes to knit and bake in her spare time. I'm hardly the prize you seem to think I am."

A slight frown creases his brow as he takes me by the hand and leads me to the edge of the bed, urging me to sit down. "Who is anyone in this world—you included—to tell me what I should see value in?"

"I—"

"I'm not finished." He touches me on the thigh and runs his fingers lightly over my skin. "I see every inch of you as pure gold, Rebecca. There isn't a thing about you I'd change, nothing I wish could be different. I just look at you and feel desire, respect, and I also feel a little undeserving."

"Undeserving?" I pull my head back. "How in the world could you be undeserving of me? Have you seen you?"

"I have. And unlike most of the people who look at me and see the money and the success, what I see when I look in the mirror is the kid nobody wanted. The kid whose mother couldn't quit drugs for. Besides Banks, you're the only other person in this world who knows those things about me, and unlike a lot of those Ivy League kids we used to work with, you didn't even flinch finding out I came from the projects, and you've never once made me feel like you were in this for my money."

"That's because I admire the level of work and dedication it takes to make a better life for yourself. My father also raised me to value time and effort more than money."

"He's a smart man. I look forward to meeting him one day."

"Yeah?"

"Absolutely."

"Good, because he wants to meet you too. I just didn't want to force that step unless you were ready."

"Oh, I'm ready. I'm serious about us, Rebecca. I want us to work. And I hope you feel that way too."

"I do," I say, staring into his blue eyes as I melt a little more on the inside. In the beginning, I wondered if this was a dream, but now that I realize this man is my reality I feel like the luckiest girl alive. "I want to build a life with you." He grins and all of a sudden I wonder if that was too much. "If that's what you want too, of course."

"I want everything with you, cashmere," he murmurs, leaning in and pressing his lips to mine in a kiss that starts out slow, but very quickly heats up as he guides me back on the bed, holding himself over me.

"Ronan." A sigh escapes my lips as he runs his hands up along my torso before grabbing both of my hands and lifting them over my head.

"Do you have any idea what you do to me? How obsessed I am thinking about little else but you, day in and day out?" he whispers into my ear before nipping lightly at the lobe. "It's almost maddening."

"I started fantasizing about you when we first met," I gasp as he grinds himself against me, his mouth gliding along the hollow of my neck. "I dreamed about you constantly."

"I hated that being near you made me feel so out of control," he whispers as his hands cup my breasts. "But I could never bring myself to send you away. The more time I spent with you, the more I needed you close."

I arch up against him as his thumbs brush over my nipples, hardening under his touch. "I've never had any control," I moan. "I'm constantly longing for your touch. Then and now. Please, Ronan. Touch me."

A soft rumble leaves his chest as he moves his mouth to my neck again, biting and sucking until I'm gasping for air. Then one of his hands moves down between my legs and I cry out as he begins to stroke me expertly. It feels so good that I can't help but writhe against him, trying to increase the pressure of his touch.

"I love to watch you come undone," he rasps, slipping his fingers past the edge of my panties and groaning when he makes contact with my slick core. "I love knowing I'm the only man doing this to you."

"You are. I couldn't imagine wanting anyone else now that I've had you. You've ruined me, Ronan."

Pressing up on his free arm, he looks down at me tenderly. "Good," he says, slipping his fingers inside me and fucking me the way he knows I like it, his thumb moving against my clit as I writhe and gasp. "Not yet, sweet girl."

Pulling his hand from my core, he hooks his fingers in the side of my panties and drags them down my legs. "Please, Ronan," I beg, reaching for him.

"Lose the bra," he instructs, getting up for the

amount of time it takes for him to step out of his boxers before he's climbing right back on top of me.

"Better?" I ask, sliding my arms around his shoulders as my oversized breasts press against his hard chest.

He groans. "Much better," he says, guiding himself inside me then dragging his length back and forth at a slow and steady pace.

"More," I gasp, greedy and needy for him.

"Soon," he whispers, leaning down and pressing soft kisses all over my face and mouth. "There's something I need to tell you first."

"Yeah?"

He stills, his cock half in and half out as he looks deep into my eyes. "I'm in love with you, Rebecca."

"You are?"

"Yeah. I haven't had a lot of good examples of it in my life to recognize it sooner, but the more I'm with you, the more I know—I'm crazy in love with you."

"I'm crazy in love with you too," I whisper, lacing my hands behind his neck as he leans in and melds his mouth with mine, kissing me and fucking me sweet and slow, then deep and hard. When we both get close, he leans back and rubs his thumb over my sensitive clit, causing me to throw my head back and howl his name so loud I'm sure that all of my neighbors can hear. But I don't care one little bit, because Ronan Kennedy is in love with me. I think I can die happy and have zero regrets now. Put a fork in me, I'm done.

BECCA

With the busiest period of my working life and burgeoning career coming up once we finalize the deal with Medican, I decide to set a night aside to spend it with Nina, who really, was the first person in my life besides my dad to put their faith in me. She supported me every step of the way when I wanted to change my life. She never judged. She was simply there for me because that's what best friends do.

They also gossip and giggle, which is exactly what Nina and I are doing as we sit in my living room finishing off a pepperoni pizza and drinking wine.

"So you're really going to do it? You're going to go back to school and get your business degree to work your way up to partner in Ronan's company?" she asks for what feels like the hundredth time, although it was likely closer to the twentieth.

"Absolutely. Ronan says he'll help me every step of

the way, and once I finish, I have a guaranteed fast track to partner. Eventually, you'll see the names Kennedy and Greer up on the wall."

"You wouldn't use Maxwell since that's the name you've been going as for a while now?"

"No." I shake my head. "I think I'd rather my dad's name goes on the wall over my mother's. It feels a little weird connecting hers to my success when she upped and left before my journey had even really started."

"That's fair. But here's another option for you to consider—what if it's Kennedy and Kennedy by then?" Nina bites her lip in a smile as she nods excitedly. "You guys are pretty serious now. Marriage could be the next step."

It's only been a couple of months of Ronan and I dating. Six months since he and I first crossed paths, so it feels too early to be thinking about wedding bells. But I'd be lying if that thought hadn't entered my mind. Actually, I think it'd be kind of cool if we were. Kennedy and Kennedy - Venture Capital. I can see the gold plaque on the wall, clear as day in my mind, but I don't dare to admit it out loud.

"That's a long way off," I say instead, reaching for my wine to hide the hopeful blush in my cheeks.

"Oh, I don't know. He seemed really smitten with you when he left earlier. I kind of felt bad making him go. It was like he was this little lost puppy, which is so weird because I've only ever known him as that stern guy who yelled at anyone who crossed him at work. You've been a calming influence on him."

"Pete said he thought I'd made him soft."

"I don't think that's true at all. Look at you two, adding massive clients to your portfolio. Give it a few years and you'll be outshining Pierce Goodman. You might even need your own admin department, one of which I'm quite capable of running."

"That would be pretty cool, actually. I'll definitely keep you in mind for it."

"I'll be sure to keep my resume updated so I'm ready for that call," she says with a giggle, taking another swig of her wine. "Maybe you could hire a really hot VC for me to fall in love with too. The pickings are rather slim out there these days. I'm about to give up on dating entirely."

I laugh, finishing off the last of my pizza. "I think you might have to kiss a lot of frogs before you find your prince."

"Ew, gross! I don't want to kiss any frogs," she says with a shudder. "That's why I've deleted all my dating apps. I'm actually thinking of becoming a member of this club I heard about."

"A club? What kind of club?"

"One where you fill out a form stating the things you do and don't like, and then they match you up with someone . . . anonymously."

"Anonymously?" I lean forward and place my glass on

the coffee table. "I don't know if I understand what you're saying."

"It's like a blind date, but you never find out who the other person is. It's about having your needs met without any of the mind games or wasted time dating. And what makes me really want to consider it is that it's completely safe. No one is allowed to break the rules or they get banned for life and outed for whatever they did. The place is literally called Blind Trust."

"That sounds . . . interesting," I say, trying to wrap my head around why my friend would want to get involved with something like that.

"I know, I know. It's a bit out there. But, I don't know . . . maybe it could work out for me. You know, get my needs met so there's no pressure to find someone who is both interesting to be around and good in bed. That combination isn't easy to find. Well, unless your name is Becca and you're plucked out of the admin pool to work for Ronan. There was a little kismet happening there. So maybe what I need to do is occupy myself until my chance at kismet comes my way."

"Well, I don't really understand what this club is all about," I say, choosing my words carefully. "But whatever decision you make, I'll support it without judgment. I really just want to see you happy. So whatever that looks like for you, you have my understanding."

"Thanks, Bec. I was kinda nervous talking about it, but I didn't want to do it without at least having someone I trust know where I'm going."

"I'm glad you came to me. And I want you to let me know what you decide, OK? I don't want you feeling like you can't call if this turns out to be something you're uncomfortable with."

"Deal. And the moment Ronan proposes, I wanna know about that too, OK? I expect to be your maid of honor."

"Deal." I laugh, clinking my glass against hers. "Even though I'm sure anything like that is a long, long way off."

"We'll see," she says, giving me a wink as she takes a long pull from her glass.

RONAN

"You keep looking at your watch, Ronan," Banks says as he deals out the cards. "Got somewhere you need to be?"

I pick up my hand and start pulling unwanted cards out to discard. "Just keeping an eye on things," I say, dropping my cards in the middle. "Give me three."

"I say he's counting down the minutes until it's time to get back home to his lady," Darren—Banks's cousin and everyone's favorite drag queen—says as he flutters his lashes over the top of his fanned-out hand.

"When are you planning on introducing us all?" Darren's fiancé, Theo, says, quirking a blond brow my way.

"Oh yes!" Darren says, bouncing up and down with excitement. "I would love to meet the woman who got the grumpiest bastard I know to start smiling and enjoying life for a change."

"Nice to see you're still a massive brat," I say, earning a poked-out tongue from my longtime friend. Darren really hasn't changed much from the gangly kid I grew up with energy-wise. He's just prettier now with his fancy nails and extra-long lashes.

"I'll bring her around soon, I promise," I add after a moment of silence.

"Promises, promises," Theo says with that look he has every time we play poker and he manages to win big. It's like he doesn't even have to try anymore. Not my kind of luck, unfortunately. I either bluff my way to a win, or I don't win at all.

"I've met her," Banks says, grinning with an air of authority as he lifts his beer and tilts it back. "She's a keeper, that one."

I arch an eyebrow in question and Banks just shrugs. "You look at her the way I imagine I used to look at Isla before we got together."

"And how's that?" I ask.

"Like you'd die if you ever had to live without her."

Something about his words hit me hard, and I quickly fold my hand, dropping it into the middle of the table. "Jesus. I'm out."

"God. You're out? You straight people are so dramatic," Darren says as the hand ends with Theo winning—again. He scoops up the cards and begins to shuffle them. "When Theo and I got together, we knew right away what we wanted and there weren't any games, no umming and ahhing over the extent of our feelings. It either was, or it wasn't. And since I have this beautiful rock on my finger." He waggles his engagement ring for us all to see. "It definitely was. So, whatever this Becca girl is to you, Ronan, work toward that the same way you would one of your business dealings. Go with your gut and don't second guess it. You'll only lose out in the end if you do."

I take a swallow of my beer and lean back in my chair, studying my friends and letting their words sink in. They've all known me for years, known me to be a good friend, a focused worker, but closed off whenever it comes to relationships. I've never been the commitment type. I'm more of a one and done kind of guy until now. And that has led to me having a lot of short-term flings, but never anything serious. But Becca is different. I can't explain it, but I know she's the one.

And Darren's right. If I want this to work, I need to go in with my eyes open. Stop overthinking things and just go for it. I don't want to waste any more time dancing around my feelings for her. I've already admitted that I love her. Now, I think it's time to take yet another step forward.

Setting my bottle down, I give Darren a smile. "You know what? You're right. I am holding back, and I am overthinking things."

"Thank you. I do tend to be right about these things," Darren says.

"He's not humble, though," Theo puts in with a chuckle.

"Well, that's because I have no reason to be," Darren

says. "I have been the relationship counsellor to every one of our straight friends. I actually think I should start charging."

"It's true," Banks says. "He gives great advice."

"I do. You should definitely take it." Darren lifts his glass of whiskey and tilts it toward me. I reciprocate with my beer. "Go ask her to marry you or something."

Beer sprays everywhere.

"Whoa! Maybe not marriage," Banks laughs, slapping me on the back as I cough and choke.

"Jesus, Darren, I can't believe you mentioned the M word around the commitment-phobe," Theo says.

"I'm not a commitment-phobe," I gasp. "I just don't want to rush into things with her and freak her out. We're already moving pretty fast."

"Don't stress it, buddy," Banks says. "You take your time. We all do these things when we're ready. And if she's the girl for you, she'll be there ready when you are."

The conversation shifts gears as Darren deals the next hand, but all I can think is that Rebecca is the girl for me. There's no doubt in my mind about that. So instead of sitting here wondering if I'm doing this all wrong, I leave my hand on the table and get up from my chair.

"Leaving already?" Banks asks.

"Yeah. You guys have given me a lot to think about, but I think the person I should be talking to is Rebecca. I'll see you all soon."

"Good luck!" Darren singsongs as I grab my coat and leave with only one destination in mind.

BECCA

*A*fter clearing away the empty pizza box and wine glasses from my evening with Nina, I twist my messy curls into a top knot and get changed into my most comfy sweatpants and sweatshirt. I'm a little too buzzed to go to sleep, so I put the Hallmark channel on and grab my knitting bag to work on the soft gray cardigan I'm making for myself since it gets a little draughty in the office at times. The plan is to keep it draped over the back of my chair so I can take it on and off depending on my comfort levels.

Just as I get into my rhythm, a knock sounds at my door. Frowning, I set my craft aside and make my way to my foyer, looking through the peephole since I didn't get a call from the concierge about a visitor. My heart leaps in my chest when I'm met with a fisheye view of my favorite person in the world—Ronan.

"What on earth are you doing here?" I gasp, throwing

the door open and practically jumping into his arms. "I thought we were spending the night apart?"

"About that," he says, a half-grin curving his mouth as he catches me about the waist and draws me to him. "I know we agreed to take things slow, and spending a healthy amount of time together and apart was part of that. But when I was sitting there talking to the guys tonight, I realized that the only thing I really wanted was to be right here with you. I don't care if it's together in bed, at work, on the couch while I read and you knit, or if we're just sitting around doing nothing at all. I just want us to be together. I want to come home to you, Rebecca."

I pull my head back slightly and grin. "Are you . . . are you suggesting we move in together?"

"I am. I feel . . . incomplete when you're not around."

"Yes," I say, a massive smile on my face as we stand there in my open doorway, looking at each other like we just won something huge. And I suppose we have. We've won each other's hearts.

"Yes? You'll move in with me—or I'll move in with you. Hey, we can even get a whole new place that we choose together."

"Yes!" I say again, tugging him into the apartment and closing the door. "I'll live with you anywhere. All I want is you."

"I love you, Rebecca." With a light brush of his thumb against my jaw, he presses his lips to mine and I completely melt against him, my world feeling complete the moment we connect. The entire world fades away, and all there is, is the feel of his body, the press of his lips on mine, and the way my heart sings at knowing he's here because he wants to be with me.

"I love you too, Ronan," I whisper. "So much."

"Mmm. Now all that's to do is for me to take you into the bedroom and pound you senseless until morning."

"Lucky it's the weekend then so I'll have some time to recuperate."

"Recuperate? No way. We're going to get up in the morning and do it all over again. In between searching for a new apartment on Zillow, of course."

I laugh against him as he sweeps me into his arms. "Deal."

RONAN

Despite conducting an extensive search of Manhattan real estate, in the end, Becca and I decided to make my brownstone our permanent residence—after a few changes, of course. So, in the months it took to get an interior designer to redecorate, we got a practice run at living together in her apartment. I'm happy to report that it was awesome. We even made it through the stress of the holidays while also packing up and sorting her things into what comes with her to the brownstone and what went to Goodwill. Yes, there were arguments. But no, I didn't yell once. Shocking since before Rebecca came into my life that was my go-to in every stressful situation. She seems to have calmed me. And even though her brother suggested that toning of my aggression made me less effective at my job, I'm here to argue the opposite. Rebecca makes me a better man.

"What time is everyone coming?" Becca asks, walking

out of our bathroom, looking amazing in a red dress that has a fitted bodice and a skirt that flares out at the hips and has me thinking about how much fun I'll have bunching that above her waist later.

"Nine," I say, checking my watch. "We have about twenty minutes."

"I'm of half a mind to call them all and cancel," she says, grinning as she moves to stand in front of where I sit on the end of the bed, ready to go downstairs with her to greet our guests. "What on earth made us think sharing our very first New Year's Eve celebration with fifty people was a good idea?"

"Oh, I don't know," I say, resting my hands on her waist as she settles hers on my shoulders. "I remember something about wanting to share our happiness with a combined housewarming, New Year's party."

"Hmm. That does sound like something I'd say. You should probably remind me of this moment right here the next time I think up something crazy like that in the future. They feel more fun in my head than I think they are in real life. In reality, I think I'd rather it just be you and me ringing in the new year wearing nothing but a smile on our faces."

"I do like the sound of that," I say, urging her closer as I tilt my head up toward her. "Maybe it isn't too late to cancel on everyone."

"Yeah?" She laughs as I bring my mouth to hers, kissing her softly but not getting too far when the ring of the doorbell announces our first guest. "Guess we missed that cancellation window after all."

I groan as I rise to my feet and press a kiss to the side of her head before taking her by the hand and heading downstairs together. We've hired caterers and waitstaff for the evening, so it's the event planner who's opening the door and letting in Becca's father, Mr. Reginald Greer.

"Dad!" Becca cries out, happy to see him. "Happy New Year!"

"Happy New Year to you too, sweetheart," he says, giving her a hug before turning to me. "And here's the man who makes my daughter smile more than I've ever seen."

"I'm honored to be the man she chooses every day, sir," I say, holding out my hand. He takes it and shakes it firmly before releasing it.

"No formalities tonight, please," he says with a smile. "Just call me Reg."

"Reg, it is," I say. "And thank you for coming. We're glad you could make it."

"Any time spent with family is worth the effort," he says before turning to Becca and giving her another hug. "Now, the invite suggested there'd be a bar of some sort. How about we pick ourselves up a glass of something and then you can show your old man around this fancy house?"

"Right this way," Becca says, rolling her eyes with a

laugh at the word 'fancy' as she ushers her dad into the living room. In the beginning, she was worried he'd look down on her for the way we threw money at the brownstone's makeover. But with Reg, it's not the money he dislikes, it's the carelessness money can bring. And the fact we've invited him and all our friends and family over for the evening to spend *time* together, is really all the man wants. Sure, time is money, but time spent with those you love is priceless. It's something the old man and I agree on.

As I watch Becca head off with her dad arm in arm, I'm reminded again of how damn lucky I am. Becca has brought more happiness into my life than I ever could have imagined, and I can't wait to see what the new year brings for us.

"I come in peace," Peter says, stepping through the door then holding his hand out to shake mine.

"I expect nothing less. What's in the past is in the past," I say, genuinely meaning it. Despite the trouble and misunderstandings caused when Becca and I left Pierce Goodman, he was a man of his word and didn't cause a single issue once it came to a head.

"I'm glad to hear you say that. But just to be sure, I come bearing gifts." Reaching into his suit jacket, he retrieves a folded card and hands it over to me.

"What's this?"

"A peace offering. Since you're now living with my sister, I wanted to give you something that can maybe help us move forward with a clean slate."

Opening the card, I find a name and a phone number inside. "Is this a potential client?"

"That is the number for the CEO of a logistics company. They're looking for backers to expand their fleet, and I figured they'd be a handy addition to your portfolio given your affiliation with Medican. They're a solid investment."

"Why aren't you going after them yourself?"

"That was the plan," he says, smiling. "But I'm slowly starting to understand why my father always insists that time and thoughtfulness are the biggest and most precious assets a man can have."

"Well, this is definitely a thoughtful gesture. I thank you."

"Friends?" He lifts his brow and holds out his hand again, but instead of shaking it, I draw him into a hug.

"How about, brothers?"

When we shift back, Pete is smirking. "Brothers? Does that mean you plan to propose to my sister tonight?"

Touching my nose, I give him a wink then show him where to get himself a drink. Then I make my way through our crowded home to find my gorgeous partner. I get stopped by Banks and his fiancée, Isla. They've recently had a baby girl, and this is the first night they've been out as a couple since the birth.

"How are you both feeling?" I ask, giving them hugs and handshakes.

"Like I forgot what's it like not to be a cow with udders," Isla says with a laugh.

"We're having a wonderful time," Banks says with a chuckle. "The place looks amazing."

"Thank you. I like how it turned out. Actually, I'm overjoyed by how the entire year panned out. Thank you for pushing me to be more."

"What's family for?" he asks, drawing Isla in closer to his side. "Everything set for midnight?"

"Sure is," I say, patting my inside pocket as I turn from my best friend and continue looking for the light of my life, checking my watch periodically so I don't miss my window.

I can't help but smile at the thought of what's to come. Tonight, when the clock strikes twelve, I'm going to ask Becca to marry me. And she's going to say yes.

After a short search, I find her in the living room talking with her friend, Nina, and showing her the big, comfy knitting chair I insisted we put in here right by the fire so we can spend many a night in quiet companionship over the years to come. She's laughing and sipping on a glass of champagne, and I find my chest swelling at the sight of her long curly hair bouncing with her movement. She sees me coming and her face lights up with a smile.

"Hey, you," she says, setting down her glass and walking into my arms. "I was just telling Nina about your argument with the designer over this chair."

Chuckling, I slide an arm around her waist and turn

my attention to Nina. "She kept saying it messed with the overall scheme, and I kept insisting she needed to make it fit. I think it worked out well."

"I have to agree," Nina says. "It fits your decor while also being entirely Becca. I can just imagine you sitting there knitting tiny booties and sweaters for all the babies you two are likely to produce."

"Nina!" Becca giggles. "We literally just moved in together. Give it some time."

Nina meets my eyes with a knowing look—she's the one who helped me get the ring sized correctly. "What is it your dad says? Time is precious and shouldn't be wasted."

"Yes, but—"

"How about we mingle a little?" I suggest, giving Nina an amused but stern look that just makes her give me a cheeky grin.

"Of course," she says, and I take Becca's hand again to lead her back out into the main room where we can hear everyone chatting amicably.

As we move, I feel like I'm walking on air. My girl is on my arm, our friends and family seem to be getting on like a house on fire, and the future looks bright. When I check my watch and see that we only have ten minutes to midnight, I give the planner the sign to make sure everyone has a glass in hand then lead Becca to the base of the stairs so I can make my toast.

"Hey everyone," I say loudly enough that they can

hear me across the room. "I just wanted to thank you all for coming out tonight."

A few people call out their thanks as well and lift their glasses in toast. After replying in kind with my own glass raised high, I continue, "This past year has been filled with some trials, but it's also held a whole lot of joy. And most of that joy has been at the hands of my beautiful girlfriend, Rebecca. She's not only challenged me professionally, but she's helped me grow personally. My future has never felt as bright as it does when she's on my arm or by my side, and it's for that reason that I want to enter this new year as something more than just boyfriend and girlfriend. I want us to be so much more than that."

Reaching into my pocket, I pull out the velvet box and lower to one knee, looking up at a now gasping Rebecca.

"What are you doing?" she practically wheezes. "Ronan! Oh my gosh."

"Rebecca," I start, taking her hand in mine after opening the box and revealing the large square solitaire set within a diamond-platinum band. "From the moment I met you, my life changed for the better. And with every day, week and month that followed, one thing became abundantly clear. I want you in my life. I need you in my life. You are the person I've always searched for, and I can't wait to build a life, a company, and to start a family of our own with you. Will you marry me?"

There's a mad rush of noise as the other guests gasp

and react to my proposal, and then it fades into a vacuum of silence. All I can see is Rebecca's face as she gazes at me with tears pooling in her eyes. Behind her, Nina is gripping Banks's arm so tightly that he winces slightly while Becca's dad and brother look on with happy grins from across the room, along with everyone else we hold dear to our hearts. There's an eternity where no one makes a sound or moves before Rebecca leans down and wraps her arms around my neck so she can press a fervent kiss to my lips. "Yes, Ronan! Yes!"

A whoop goes up from everyone still standing nearby, I barely have time to put my ring on Rebecca's finger when the countdown begins, but somehow—as it always does when I'm with her—our kiss is the only thing that matters. All of this means everything to me because she's made it all possible. Everything else is just icing on an already perfect cake.

When I met Rebecca, I was known as the jerk of Wall St. But now, almost a year later, I'm sure the jerk title is long gone. Now, I'm known as the luckiest bastard on Wall St. because she's mine. She said yes. And we're going to live happily ever after. I just know it.

EPILOGUE

Becca

five years later...

What's a babymoon? I hear you ask. Well, it's a last vacation before the baby arrives. But this is more than just a trip to the Caribbean or a long weekend out of town. The idea is to give expecting parents some time away from their normal everyday lives, and it's to be relaxing and rejuvenating—two things that are quite difficult with an infant in tow, and even more difficult when you've spent the last five years studying and building a successful business with your husband. With every step that Ronan and I have taken forward, we've always known it would change our lives. But we also knew it would bring us closer together. So as we prepare to say goodbye to coupledom and hello to diapers and late night feedings, we're feeling excited and certain that together, this new challenge will be yet another wild ride in the life of us. We're also really enjoying our holiday too!

"Do you think we could successfully run the business from a hut on the beach?" I ask Ronan, lying on a banana chair on a floating bamboo pontoon outside our little home away from home. "I kind of like this lazing about by the water watching the sun go down business."

He peers at me over his glasses and smirks. "If the only businesses you want to back are hotels and souvenir stores, then sure, we could make it work."

I giggle and lean back to watch the red sun sink into the sea. "You know, I honestly think that with you at the helm, that *would* work."

"You give me too much credit," he says, leaning over and kissing me on my forehead with a chuckle. "We are successful because *we* make a great team. And Scott is OK too."

"He gets better with every year," I say, laughing as he pulls me up for a dance as Latin music floats out from our hut.

"He does. And the fact we can trust him to run things while we're away is a great load off my mind."

"Helps that Banks is always a phone call away too," I say, lacing my hands behind his neck. It feels nice to just sway together in our own little cocoon of love and not worry about life's many responsibilities that are constantly snapping at our heels with their sharp incisors.

"We have wonderful people surrounding us."

"How did we get so lucky?"

"I think it happened when we found each other," he says, his gaze warm. "Everything just kind of fell into place from there."

"You're right," I say, lifting up on my toes and meeting his mouth with mine. We come together, both knowing that our lives will be changing even more soon but neither one of us feeling any trepidation. Couple time is rare these days anyway after building up Kennedy & Kennedy—yes, my name went on the wall the very day I got my MBA—over the last five years, so adding a little one into the mix won't change that a lot. Especially since we've both agreed to relax our work hours a little to share the parenting load. Since Ronan never knew his father, he has great plans to be a very involved dad. We may have all the money in the world, but as we've all heard enough from my dad at this point, money doesn't replace love, so Ronan wants to make sure he gives his child as much love and *time* as possible.

"What are you thinking about?" Ronan murmurs against my lips.

"Just how happy I am." I smile through our kiss, pulling away just long enough to look at him with a heavy sigh. "It's been a great five years."

"It has," he agrees, his eyes never once leaving mine before he kisses me again.

And it really has been. After our engagement, I enrolled in college and got my MBA, all while working and learning on the job, helping Ronan and Scott run things and organizing a wedding to boot. Sure, I had help from a planner in the wedding department, but it was still a massive effort, and I'm so damn proud of both Ronan and I for pulling together in all instances to get our life to the point it is today. The business is doing great, I'm pregnant with our first child, and I'm married to the love of my life. Add to that the fact I'm having a wonderful time on our babymoon—probably our last holiday for quite some time . . . at least until all the kids we plan on having are old enough to come along too—and you have something pretty close to perfection. Ronan and I are moving into the next stage of our lives, and though it's scary in some ways, we know that everything will work out just fine. As long as we have each other, nothing can bring us down.

"Ready to head inside, Mrs. Kennedy?" Ronan asks, his tongue doing that thing with the shell of my ear that he knows curls my toes. "I've got some dessert I plan on eating off your body."

"Don't need to ask me twice," I say, practically chasing him back into our cabin and jumping onto the bed naked.

And as we make love while the sun disappears from view, I can't help but feel grateful for everything Ronan and I have found in each other. We've worked hard and overcome obstacles to get to this point in our lives, and we've never lost sight of each other or of those who are important to us. And even in our darkest times, this journey has been worth every minute. Now that we're about to embark on the next big adventure—parenthood—I know that since we'll be bringing more strong-willed Kennedy's into the world, we're in for a rather exciting ride.

Look out world, look out Wall Street, the best is yet to come . . .

THE END.... *ISH*

If you're not quite ready to let go of Becca, Ronan and the gang, Wall St. Rascal will see a return of some of your favorites. Nina, perhaps? I wonder how she fares after joining that 'Blind Trust' club she's interested in?

Speaking of interest, if you're interested in getting yourself a FREE royal romance, you can join my newsletter >>HERE<< and get yourself a cute, squishy, fun read.

But, if you hate joining lists and just want to be notified whenever I have a new release, click 'follow' on Amazon when the rating window pops up on your device.

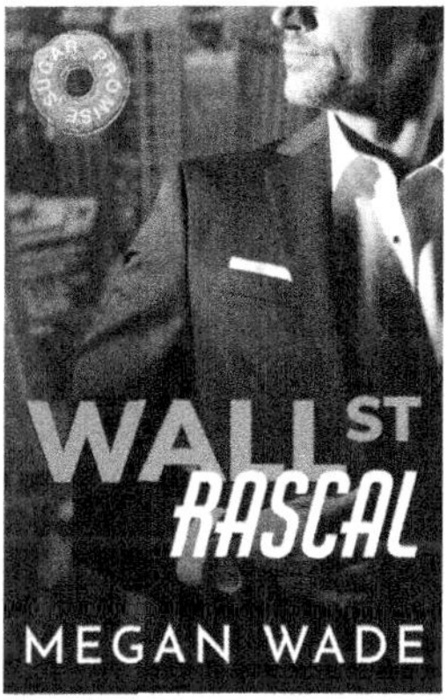
SUGAR PROMISE
WALL ST
RASCAL
MEGAN WADE

ALSO BY MEGAN WADE

Novels

Standalones

Mine for the Holidays

Wrong/Wright Series

Wrong Car, Wright Guy

Wrong Room, Wright Girl

Wrong Place, Wright Time

The Curves of Wall St.

Wall St Jerk

Wall St. Rascal

Novellas

Hermits & Curves Series

Sunshine & the Recluse

Cocktails & Curves Series

Swipe for a Cosmo

Old Fashioned Sweetie

Dark & Stormy Darlin'

Cute as a Lemon Drop

Happy Curves Series

Sheets & Giggles

Quilts & Chuckles

Sweet Curves Series

Marshmallow

Pumpkin

Pop

Sugarplum

Cookie

Sucker

Taffy

Toffee Apple

Peaches & Cream

Cupcake

Cheesecake

Wedded Curves Series

Whoa! I married a Mountain Man!

Whoa! I married a Billionaire!

Whoa! I married the Pitcher!

Whoa! I Married a Rock Star!

Whoa! I Married a Biker!

Sugar Curves

Sugar Honey Ice Tea

Yikes on a Cracker

What the Hell-o Kitty-Kat

Horse's Ask

Holy Cannoli

Hells Bells & Taco Shells

Holy Frozen Snowcones

Son of a Nutcracker

Curves Just Wanna Have Fun

Half Baked

Deep, Deep Donuts

Unexpected Sweetheart

Drink it Down

Sweet Ride

The Not So Silent Night

Cillian

Collaborations

518 Hope Ave (Cherry Falls)

GET IN TOUCH WITH MEGAN WADE

Megan Wade is a simple girl who believes in love at first sight and soulmates. She's obsessed with happy endings and Hallmark is her favorite brand of everything. Each Megan Wade story carries her 'Sugar Promise' of Over the Top Romance, Alpha Heroes, Curvy Heroines, Low Drama, High Heat and a Guaranteed Happily Ever After. What could be better than that?

email: contact@meganwadebooks.com

Newsletter: Get a copy of Rowdy Prince FREE when you sign up and confirm: https://www.subscribepage.com/meganwade_freebie

Amazon follow: click 'follow' on Amazon when the

rating window pops up on your device so the kindle app will notify you of new releases.

Facebook: https://www.facebook.com/meganwadeauthor/

Sweeties group: https://www.facebook.com/groups/959211654464973

Instagram: https://www.instagram.com/meganwadewrites/

Printed in Great Britain
by Amazon